# "Get down," Kirk ordered.

Stasi's eyes widened as she looked at him. What *was* happening? Were Kirk's actions related to the attack? She already doubted she could trust the man. He'd been linked to such a horrible crime before.

"Down," Kirk commanded, his open palm pushing her head below the level of the dashboard.

She grabbed his wrist and tore his arm away from her royal head. "No. I won't do what you say."

Kirk stopped the Jeep with a jerk and glared at her. "Don't fight me. Don't you see? The royal family has been attacked. If anyone sees you, they'll know you weren't killed. I've got to get you out of here."

Stasi looked at him dumbly. Too much didn't make sense. "What do you mean? You think someone might try to kill me?"

"Please." Kirk's voice plunged to pleading depths. "You've got to stay down. Your life is in danger."

Stasi shrunk in her seat, but her eyes didn't leave Kirk's face. "What are you going to do with me?"

"I'm going to hide you, if I can." He looked around at the empty streets. "But you've got to do what I say."

## Books by Rachelle McCalla

Love Inspired Suspense

*Survival Instinct*
*Troubled Waters*
*Out on a Limb*
*Danger on Her Doorstep*
*Dead Reckoning*
\*Princess in Peril
\*Protecting the Princess

\*Reclaiming the Crown

## RACHELLE McCALLA

is a mild-mannered housewife, and the toughest she
ever has to get is when she's trying to keep her four
kids quiet in church. Though she often gets in over
her head, as her characters do, and has to find a way
out, her adventures have more to do with sorting
out the carpool and providing food for the potluck.
She's never been arrested, gotten in a fistfight or
been shot at. And she'd like to keep it that way!
For recipes, fun background notes on the places and
characters in this book and more information on
forthcoming titles, visit www.rachellemccalla.com.

# PROTECTING
## THE PRINCESS

### RACHELLE
### McCALLA

*Love Inspired*

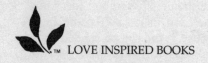

LOVE INSPIRED BOOKS

Recycling programs
for this product may
not exist in your area.

ISBN-13: 978-0-373-44478-6

PROTECTING THE PRINCESS

www.LoveInspiredBooks.com

**Printed in U.S.A.**

On the Sabbath we went outside the city gate to the river, where we expected to find a place of prayer. We sat down and began to speak to the women who had gathered there. One of those listening was a woman named Lydia, a dealer in purple cloth from the city of Thyatira, who was a worshiper of God. The Lord opened her heart to respond to Paul's message. When she and the members of her household were baptized, she invited us to her home. "If you consider me a believer in the Lord," she said, "come and stay at my house." And she persuaded us.
—*Acts* 16:13–15

To Eleanor, my princess,
who taught me to wear pink and enjoy jewelry.
You are stronger than you think you are. I love you.

## Acknowledgments

Thank you to my loving and supportive family,
who insist they enjoy frozen pizza, freeing me
from cooking so I can write. I love you all!

Thanks also to my awesome friends
whose insights contributed to the factual accuracy
of this book. Special thanks to Lonny Douthit,
my cousin who flies helicopters, who patiently tried to
explain them to me. Any errors are mine, not his!
And to all the friends who chimed in on my efforts
to name the Crown Prince—because of you, he is not
Xerxes or Phineas or Arthur. Thank you. And let me
not forget all those friends who supplied terms
and words when my brain ran dry. Because of you,
the-woman-behind-the-ticket-counter-who-sells-
tickets-at-the-airport shall henceforth be known as
a ticketing agent. Ah. So much better.

And special thanks to my editor extraordinaire,
Emily Rodmell, for her insight, expertise and patience
with my frantic Friday afternoon email barrages.
Enjoy your weekend in peace, you've earned it!

Disclaimer: The people and events of this story are
fiction. There is no nation of Lydia, although there
was a woman named Lydia mentioned in Acts chapter
16 of the Bible, and she had a house church in that
area of the world. Beyond that, this story is the fruit of
my imagination, and any resemblance to
any persons living or dead is purely coincidental.

# ONE

Her Royal Highness Princess Anastasia of Lydia grabbed the doorknob and gave it a turn, but when she tried to push the door open, it wouldn't budge.

Stasi blinked. How strange! Her door had never given her any problems before. She tried again, this time pushing harder, but with no success. Finally, throwing all her weight into it, she shoved the door with her shoulder. Nothing.

Had someone barricaded her door so it wouldn't open?

Stasi looked around her suite uneasily.

She was trapped inside her own room, and the royal motorcade would be leaving any minute for the state dinner.

Refusing to give in to the panic she felt, Stasi grabbed her phone and dialed the number for the palace managers.

Theresa Covington answered.

"I'm trapped inside my room—and the motorcade is leaving any second!" She fingered her sapphire necklace uneasily.

"I'll send someone immediately."

"Thank you." Stasi ended the call and waited, glancing nervously around, wondering why her door wouldn't open, and if the peculiar disturbance had anything to do with the other unusual trespasses she'd experienced lately. She knew of at least three other times in the past few weeks when items in her room had been eerily displaced—not stolen outright, but disturbed, as though they'd been rooted through, and then put back slightly out of order.

Footsteps approached from the hallway outside her door. "Your Highness?" A voice sounded from the other side, and she watched the doorknob turn. "Your Highness?"

"Yes!" She practically threw the door open, prepared to thank whoever had rescued her, but she startled backward when she recognized the man on the other side of the door.

Kirk Covington.

So, Theresa had sent her son.

"Thank you." Stasi glanced at the chair Kirk had pushed aside. Had it been propped against her door, preventing her from getting out? She didn't have time to analyze what had happened, so she brushed brusquely past him and hurried down the wide marble staircase. Dashing as quickly as she dared in her high heels across the gracious foyer, she flung herself through the front palace doors and blinked.

The twenty-foot-tall wrought-iron gates closed behind the last of the royal limousines a hundred meters away.

Her stomach sank.

The royal motorcade had left without her! She bit her lip, ready to cry after the ordeal of the last few minutes.

"Your Highness?" Kirk had followed her down the stairs. "Have they gone?"

"Yes." She straightened her posture to royal perfection. It wouldn't do to let Kirk Covington see her distressed.

"I'll drive you."

Stasi froze.

"I can drive myself. I'm a perfectly capable driver." She hoisted up the fluffy skirt of her long evening gown as she stepped outside and descended the palace steps.

"Yes, I suppose you *could* drive yourself—" Kirk kept pace with her, hauling an enormous military-style duffel bag over his shoulder, as if he'd been en route to somewhere when his mother sent him to free her from her room "—but then what are you going to do with your car once you arrive at the state dinner? There won't be valet parking, and if you have to hunt for a space…"

"Fine." She didn't let him get any further, but glanced at the bag he carried as they ducked into the garage. "You're sure it's no trouble?" Stasi didn't want to spend any more time in Kirk's presence, but she *had* to catch up to the rest of her family in the motorcade.

"None at all."

"Then, thank you. Which car shall we take?"

"The Jeep." He placed his thumb against the touch pad of the cabinet that housed the keys to the royal vehicles. When his thumbprint registered, a green light illuminated, and Kirk opened the cabinet, pulling out the keys and snapping the cabinet locked shut again. "Come on." He jogged past several other vehicles and empty bays to the waiting Jeep, tossing the large duffel bag he'd been carrying into the backseat.

Stasi hoisted her skirt and hurried after him, climbing into the passenger seat just as Kirk got the vehicle into gear. Worries swirled in her head, but she did her best to quiet them.

So what if Kirk Covington had been accused of murdering her brother Thaddeus, the heir to the throne of Lydia, six years before? He'd been best friends with her brother forever before that, and there had never been enough evidence to prove he'd committed any crime. Her brother's body had never been found. Kirk had been eventually been cleared of all charges and reinstated to his position as part of the royal guard. Kirk was innocent, wasn't he?

Besides, what could possibly happen on the way to the state dinner?

For most of her life, Kirk had been a trusted friend. She still didn't believe he was a dangerous man, or that he'd ever done anything to hurt her brother. But she was nearly certain he knew more of what had happened to Thaddeus than what he'd confessed. Regardless of the real facts, Kirk had been the most hated man in Lydia for the last six years. If she was seen with him, she'd never live it down.

Kirk pressed the button to open the side gates of the palace courtyard. "We'll take Mursia Street as far as State Street. I should be able to get right up beside the motorcade at the intersection. You can hop out and catch up with your family. No one has to see you arrive with me." He seemed to anticipate her reservations as the Jeep rattled down the narrow cobblestone road.

"Excellent." Stasi fumbled with her seat belt and tried to tell herself not to be so nervous. She'd be fine. From the vantage point of the high road, she could just catch a glimpse of the motorcade ahead of them as the buildings and alleyways flashed by. Much as she wanted to prompt him to hurry, she knew Kirk was driving as quickly as the narrow streets would allow. And though the pedestrians were few on the side street, it wouldn't be safe to travel too fast.

"Who barricaded your door?" Kirk asked as they bounced along.

"I don't know."

"Was it a prank?"

"I don't think so." The only people who had ever played pranks on her had been Thaddeus and Kirk, but that had been years ago. "It might be related to the other break-ins I've had lately."

"What other break-ins?" Kirk paused at a stop sign and met her eyes. He looked startled.

"Weren't you briefed on them?" As a member of the royal guard, Kirk should have been made aware of each incident report.

"I haven't heard a peep about anything having to do with you or your room. Was anything stolen?"

"Oddly enough, no. I keep careful track of all my jewelry—that's why I noticed things had been moved. But nothing was missing."

Kirk's eyes returned to the road. They were catching up to the motorcade—just in time.

Stasi tried to suppress the tremble in her voice. "Someone has been in my room before. Things have been moved. I spoke with Viktor Bosch directly." As the head of the royal guard, Viktor had insisted on handling the incidents himself.

Before Stasi could sort it out, Kirk shifted gears again as they paused at another stop sign. "We're almost there."

Stasi took advantage of their position to crane her neck, looking to where the motorcade would be passing by.

How strange.

She placed a tentative hand on Kirk's arm and pointed down the angular bend of road to where the motorcade sat.

"They're not moving. Why aren't they moving?"

Kirk's warm hazel eyes met hers for just a second, and she saw sincere fear there.

Something was terribly wrong. There were still several more blocks to go before the first limousine would reach the State House. And the royal motorcade never stopped until it reached its destination.

An ear-piercing squeal rent the clear evening, and Stasi's fingers tightened around Kirk's arm instinctively. With a loud explosion, an orange ball of fire erupted above the front of the motorcade.

Right where her parents' car had paused.

Though buildings blocked her sight of the spot, Anastasia had little doubt the massive fireball had erupted from the head limousine, or very close to it.

"No." Her lips trembled. "No. No." She shook her head in disbelief.

As though to reinforce the reality of the situation, another furious explosion rocked the earth, this time closer to the rear of the motorcade.

But her brother, Prince Alexander, and her sister, Princess Isabelle, would be riding toward the rear of the motorcade.

Right where the blast had struck.

Another bright ball of fire seared the sky.

Kirk punched the vehicle into gear and whipped the Jeep into a tight turn.

"What are you doing? What's going on?" Stasi couldn't believe the horrific sight she'd just witnessed—was still witnessing, as another loud explosion rocked the city behind them.

"Get down," Kirk ordered.

Stasi's eyes widened as she looked at him. What *was* happening? Were Kirk's actions related to the attack? He'd been linked to such a horrible crime before.

"Down!" Kirk's open palm pushed her head below the level of the dashboard.

She grabbed his wrist and tore his arm away from her royal head. "No. I won't do what you say."

Kirk stopped the Jeep with a jerk and glared at her. "Don't fight me. Don't you see? The royal family has been attacked. If anyone sees you, they'll know you weren't killed. I've got to get you out of here."

Stasi looked at him dumbly. Too many disturbing things had happened that day. "What do you mean? You think someone might try to kill me?"

Throwing a glance in the direction of the motorcade, Kirk leaned close to her ear. His voice rumbled in low tones. "I've heard rumors." Kirk was a sentinel in the royal guard. Stasi wondered if that was where the rumors he'd heard had originated. "I didn't think there was any substance to it. Clearly I was wrong."

"Rumors of what? This attack?"

Kirk's hazel eyes closed as another blast rent the air. Pain struggled across his face. When he opened his eyes, his tone was patient, yet intense. "An insurgent uprising. A coup to overthrow your father's government. Assassinating the royal family."

"My family?" Stasi could barely muster the words. She felt as though her breath had been stolen.

"Please." Kirk's voice plunged to pleading depths. "You've got to stay down. Your life is in danger."

Stasi shrunk in her seat, but her eyes didn't leave Kirk's face. "What are you going to do with me?"

"I'm going to hide you if I can." He looked around at the empty streets. "But you've got to do what I say."

Numbly, Stasi nodded, hardly able to believe what she was agreeing to. But really, she had no choice. She'd have to trust the man who'd been accused of killing her brother.

When Stasi all but disappeared into the pouf of her royal gown on the floor of his Jeep, Kirk tossed his canvas military duffel bag on top of her and prayed no one would stop them. The open Jeep offered little in the way of cover, and now that the loud explosions had ceased, the people who had rushed inside at the first sign of trouble began to peek curiously out of the buildings they passed.

Kirk took back roads to the marina. The attack shocked him, but he'd always been a man of action. He'd find a way to get the princess to safety, then come back and ask questions. Besides, it was likely too soon for anyone to know why the attacks had happened or who was behind them.

He slowed their vehicle as they approached the marina and found an out-of-the-way parking spot not far from the rocky cliffs. It was still a long trek to his sailboat, but that stage of the trip didn't worry him nearly as much as what he was about to do.

Killing the engine, Kirk leaned over and lifted the duffel bag just enough to allow him to see Stasi's frightened blue eyes looking up at him.

"We're at the marina." He laid out the bare facts of the situation. "There aren't too many people around. I'm going to take you to my boat."

He watched indecision war across her face. Would she trust him? Given the accusations that had been made against him in the past, he knew she'd have every right not to trust him. But she also had no other alternative, and he'd have to have her cooperation if he was going to get her out of the city alive.

And he *had* to get her out of the city. As a sentinel in the royal guard, he'd taken a vow to protect the royal family. There was no doubt in his mind that every minute she stayed in Sardis, her life was in greater danger.

"How am I going to get to the boat without anyone seeing me?"

Her question was an excellent one. With her golden-blond hair, inherited from her American mother, Princess Anastasia would easily stand out among the mostly darker-haired Lydians at the marina, especially since her dramatic curls were styled in an elaborate formal hairdo.

He couldn't risk letting anyone even suspect the princess was with him. He was certain her life would depend upon that.

"I'll carry you. You'll fit in my duffel bag." The enormous military-size bag was meant to carry everything a soldier needed during deployment. It was more than big enough for the petite princess.

Her mouth dropped open, and her head peeked up higher.

Kirk looked around warily. So far no one was paying them any attention. The explosions would have been clearly visible from the marina, and most of those milling about appeared to be caught up in discussions, or on the phone, staring toward the place where the smoke still rose, gesturing toward the plumes, no doubt trying to determine what had happened.

Fortunately, though the Jeep he'd driven belonged to the royal household, there was nothing about the vehicle to identify it as such. And nimble Jeeps were common enough on the steep terrain and narrow streets of Sardis, Lydia's capital city.

Unfortunately, plenty of folks, including the royal guards who'd been standing at the gates, had surely seen the princess riding with him as they left the palace. If anyone wanted to locate her, they wouldn't have to ask around long before they figured out she was with him. He would have to hurry if he was going to get her out of Sardis before anyone caught up to them.

Reluctance filled her face, but to her credit, the princess didn't protest his plan. She ducked low while he emptied the canvas bag of what he could—his royal guard uniform and some books. These he stowed in the locked compartment under the rear seat. The key to the compartment was on the key ring he'd taken from the cabinet.

"Can you wriggle in there?" He settled the open military duffel over Stasi's head.

The petite princess fumbled inside the oversize bag, and Kirk hopped out, circling around to her side of the Jeep and helping her tuck her feet inside before carefully upending the bag with her in it, and tucking the folds of her dress in after her.

Fearful eyes watched him pull the zipper up toward her face. He could see a hundred questions on her lips and knew she had to be afraid. Of the insurgents, and also, of him.

"I'll keep you safe."

She gave a tiny nod, and he zipped the bag closed.

Hefting the strap over his shoulder, he carried her as gently as he could without making a show of it. He tossed his head back and tried to look carefree as he made his way toward the boardwalk.

The youngest member of the Royal House of Lydia had always been light. This wasn't the first time he'd carried her. Growing up best friends with her elder brother, Thaddeus, Kirk had spent most of his childhood playing with the royal siblings: Thaddeus, Alexander, Isabelle and Anastasia. He'd always had a soft spot for tiny Stasi, born almost two months premature, who'd tried so hard to keep up with the older children.

While the royal siblings seemed content to run on without her, Kirk had never been willing to leave her behind. From the time he was seven and she was old enough to hold on, somewhere around the age of two, she'd been an almost constant fixture perched atop his shoulders as they'd played games in the royal garden, or gone zipping through the halls of the royal palace.

That had been years ago, before her brother's disappearance had turned the royal family and most of the Kingdom of Lydia against him. Many Lydians, the king and queen included, doubted he'd actually killed Thaddeus or even been witness to his accidental death, but he'd still gone on trial—most likely in an attempt to pressure him to reveal Thad's whereabouts since the body had never been found. Once the jury had found him not guilty for lack of evidence, he'd been untouchable, and a judge had ordered him back to his post in the royal guard.

He wasn't welcome there. He was tolerated at best, either by those who hated him for not revealing where their future king had gone, or by those who were jealous of all the media attention he'd been shown, his picture splashed across every newspaper for almost two years before the matter was settled.

He hadn't carried Stasi in far longer than those six years, but she still felt light as he tried to remove her from the danger in Sardis. Kirk shuddered to think what may have become of the royal family. Somehow, the explosions that had rocked the royal world on its edge had tipped his back into alignment. He now had a chance to prove himself to them— to demonstrate, beyond any doubt, that he would do anything to protect them. More than that, he could show them that he would never have committed the crime he'd been accused of.

At the sight of trouble up ahead, Kirk neither slowed nor rushed his steps. He drew nearer to a Lydian soldier who patrolled the marina.

The man held out his Uzi like a crossing guard beam. "Kirk Covington?"

"Yes." Kirk was used to folks he didn't know recognizing him. Though his picture didn't fill the papers as much these days, his name still landed in the tabloids often enough. People either loved or hated him. Most of those associated with the royal family fell into the latter group, and Kirk got the sense this soldier was one of them. But his experience with the media had taught him to stay one step ahead of those who might question him.

Before the soldier could ask him anything, Kirk leaned a little closer to the man. "Do you know anything about those explosions up on the hill?"

The man seemed to weigh his answer. "There's been some sort of attack. They may be locking down the city shortly."

"Ah." Kirk nodded. "Then I suppose if I'm going to get away for the weekend, I'll have to take my boat out now."

The soldier seemed to shuffle in place. Kirk got the sense he didn't really know what was going on, but the man was certainly keyed up over what had happened. He needed to get moving before the soldier thought to question him further.

"I won't keep you." Kirk tipped his head to the soldier and stepped around him.

He continued down the pier to where his sailboat sat in the water. Behind him, he heard the static buzz of the soldier's radio, and his ears pricked up at an urgent-sounding transmission, though he couldn't make out any words.

But at the soldier's confirmation back, Kirk picked up his pace. Were they on to him? Had someone spotted him leaving the palace with the princess and alerted the soldier already?

A second later the soldier shouted back at him, confirming his worst fears.

"Kirk Covington? I need to ask you some questions."

Kirk broke into a run. Slim as his odds seemed of making sail before the soldier caught up to him, he *couldn't* let anyone find the princess. If the massive explosions and the rumors he'd heard were any indication, all the members of the royal family had been targeted for assassination.

Boots pounded down the pier behind him. The man was armed. Kirk couldn't risk drawing his fire—not with the princess slung over his back.

He set the duffel down behind him on the pier and turned to face the soldier just as the man flung himself through the air toward him.

# TWO

With a roar, Kirk leaped at the man, catching him by the arms, mindful of the soldier's gun that could send a deadly spray of bullets across the pier with a touch of the trigger.

He couldn't let the man get a shot off. Stasi was far too vulnerable tucked inside his duffel bag. At the same time, Kirk realized he needed to get rid of this soldier quickly. No doubt there were others in the area. The last thing he needed to do was draw the attention of more of them.

Overpowering the man's grip on the gun through the sheer advantage of his strength, Kirk pried the weapon from the soldier's hands and flung it through the air. It splashed into the sea.

The man's hands flew to his sidearm.

Kirk jabbed his knee between the soldier's hand and his holster before he could reach his gun. Eager to end their scuffle as quickly as possible, Kirk shoved the man backward, sending him tumbling face-first into the Mediterranean. Weighed down as he was by his munitions, Kirk figured it would take the soldier a while pull himself out of the sea, though the water wasn't quite deep enough to drown in. The soldier would be fine.

Unwilling to spare even a split second to see how long it took his attacker to surface, Kirk grabbed the duffel bag and bounded toward his sloop, setting the bag that held Stasi gently down on the deck, unfettering the boat, shoving off with a mighty heave and powering up the trolling motor that would propel the boat until he could pick up a breeze in the open sea.

Navigating the lightweight craft through the crowded marina, Kirk focused on putting some distance between his boat and the soldier. He glanced back in time to see the uniformed man swimming toward a pier support. Kirk hoped he'd have to struggle to climb out of the sea in his heavy gear—that would at least buy him a little more time. And he prayed the man hadn't gotten a decent look at his boat.

Once he'd maneuvered his sailboat into the open sea, Kirk hauled the duffel into the boat's small cabin and pulled back the zipper.

The fluffy folds of Stasi's royal skirt didn't budge.

Was she okay? She hadn't suffocated in there, had she?

"Your Highness?" He pushed back the flouncy fabric, and Stasi peeled her hands from her face and blinked up at him. She was trembling, from her shoulders to her lower lip, to the tears that shimmered on her cheeks.

"Are you okay?"

She hiccupped.

Kirk wished there was something more he could do for her—some way to comfort her or dry her tears, but there wasn't time. Any number of folks might have seen him leaving the harbor. "I'm sorry." The words seemed so inadequate against the terrors they'd both just witnessed. Had her family members all been killed?

"Where are we?" Her voice shook as she disentangled herself from the inside of the bag.

"At sea. You're safe for now. I need to go back up and steer. You stay below. We can't risk anyone seeing you."

She opened her mouth as if to speak, but Kirk didn't have

time for her questions. Instead, he turned and went back above, closing the cabin door behind him. She appeared to be overcome with fear and shock, and he prayed she'd be okay until he got her to relative safety. Then he'd do what he could to reassure her.

But not now. She had to stay out of sight for now. Sardis Bay tended to be crowded. He needed to be where he could steer the craft through the busy waters.

The nation of Lydia shared the Mediterranean coast with Albania and Greece. Her capital city of Sardis was also her primary port. Beyond the marina, the cove of Sardis Bay was protected on the north by a finger of land that jutted toward an archipelago. Tourists and Lydians alike loved the white-sand beaches that rimmed the small islands, which extended for almost fifty kilometers beyond the mainland.

The islands had once formed a peninsula that was connected to the capital city, and centuries before, the royal family had built a stronghold on the rocky promontory at its tip. Now the ruins of that fortress lay at the outermost tip of the stretch of islands. No one ever ventured to the Island of Dorsi.

Dorsi was said to have been contaminated by land mines during the world wars, though no one could ever agree what enemy had placed them, since Lydia had remained neutral throughout those conflicts. Besides that, the massive blocks of limestone that teetered in ruinous towers were rumored to fall at the slightest provocation, especially when disturbed by those who didn't belong there.

The island itself was such a formidable rock that there didn't seem to be any decent spot to anchor, and if that weren't deterrent enough, the periphery of the island was dotted every twenty feet or so with fearsome signs, warning potential visitors of certain death should they venture there.

Kirk would take an indirect route to the Island of Dorsi.

If anyone tried to follow him, he could hopefully lose them among the islands, especially with evening coming on. The evasive measures would take time, and it would likely be sundown by the time he and the princess arrived on the Island of Dorsi. He could only pray they would arrive safely.

Anastasia slumped down on one of the cushioned benches that lined the sides of the boat's cabin. The summer evening was warm, but she still felt a distinct chill and hugged herself while she tried to bite back the tears that threatened to fall.

Terror squeezed her heart. She'd heard enough of Kirk's encounter with the soldier at the pier to realize they'd come quite close to being discovered. She hadn't even been certain, until he'd zipped back enough of the bag for her to see out, that she hadn't fallen into the hands of those who'd targeted her family.

At the mere thought of her family, her heart clenched. What had happened to her parents and siblings? The explosions had been so huge, the black smoke so thick, it was difficult to imagine that they might have escaped unscathed. Had they perished in the attack?

The horrifying thought was more than she could bear, and she reeled as fearsome thoughts washed over her. What would become of her family? Was she the only member of the Royal House of Lydia who'd survived? What if the assassins tracked her down? Where could she possibly go from here, alone and hunted?

When Kirk had zipped her into his bag, she'd felt a helplessness unlike anything she'd ever felt before. Though the extralarge military duffel had allowed sufficient room for her petite frame, she'd realized as Kirk carried her toward his boat that she was completely at his mercy. What if anything happened to him? What if his motives weren't pure?

Stasi thought back to the days following her brother's disappearance. Her mother, Queen Elaine had been frantic. Her father, King Philip, had insisted that Thaddeus would check in anytime—that he'd simply needed some time to himself. But as the hours had grown into days, it had become obvious that the crown prince wasn't coming home. Kirk Covington had been the last person to see him alive. Witnesses had watched the two of them take off in Kirk's boat one morning. Kirk had returned that evening alone, and had remained tight-lipped about what had happened to Thaddeus, where he was or whether he was even alive.

Kirk had been the only person of interest throughout the investigation. Thad and Kirk, both strong young men with fiery personalities, had been known to get into fights before. Stasi recalled their wrestling matches growing up. Thaddeus had always been a tad bigger than Kirk, being six months older, but Kirk had been more ruthless, and the more tenacious fighter.

The prosecution had argued Kirk and Thad had fought, that Kirk had underestimated his own strength and accidentally killed the heir to the throne, then covered up his death. But after a lengthy trial, there hadn't been enough evidence to convict him of the crime. He'd been ordered back to his post as a sentinel with the royal guard, and was untouchable after that.

The memories swirled in her mind, the betrayal she'd felt when she'd first heard Kirk had been involved with her brother's disappearance and possible death. Her brother had trusted Kirk. *She'd* trusted Kirk, looked up to him, adored him, even more than she'd adored her older brother. She'd begged him for answers, but every time she'd questioned him, he'd simply said, "I've told you all I can."

But he hadn't ever told her anything.

What if he *had* sailed off with her brother and killed him?

Were the rumors true? Was she even now in the same boat her brother had been in?

Just as terror began to choke her and waves of sorrow wash over her, Kirk poked his head into the dark cabin. The sinking sun outlined his broad shoulders. "You can come out now if you keep your head down."

"Okay." Her voice wobbled, but she held back her tears and stood. At the very least she wanted to see where they were and where Kirk was taking her.

She'd kicked off her high-heeled shoes and now followed him barefoot onto the deck, the hem of her long gown brushing against her toes. The little boat dipped among the gentle waves, and Stasi had to focus on keeping her legs steady.

The first stars twinkled in the eastern sky, so much brighter out at sea than they ever were in the city. The red light of the setting sun spilled like blood across the western sky, coloring the sea, and Stasi tried not to read it as an omen of her family's fate.

Shuffling forward to stand near Kirk at the prow, she tried to evaluate their position, but between the darkening sky and her tear-blurred vision she could hardly see anything. In the dark of the boat's cabin, the horror of what she'd seen on the streets of Sardis had seemed so far away, like a scene from a movie, like something she could walk away from when the lights came on.

But out here on the deck, with the same balmy breeze that had warmed her when the first blast had struck the motorcade, the reality didn't seem so distant, the bloodred waters painting too vivid an image of what may have happened. Her stomach lurched with the rocking of the boat.

"You're holding together well," Kirk observed.

Stasi tried to nod, but a spasm of loss and terror clenched at her stomach. Was her family gone? Were they dead? All of them? As the boat rocked up and then down, Stasi leaned over the side, losing what was left of her lunch into the sea.

A moaning sob escaped her lips.

"It's all right." Kirk grabbed a towel from somewhere.

Stasi wanted to correct him, to assure him that nothing was right, or ever would be again, but all she could do was grab the low rail that edged the side of the boat, gagging and heaving nothing from her empty stomach.

"You'll be all right." He dabbed the corners of her mouth with the towel before she leaned forward and retched dry air toward the salt sea.

She shook her head and gasped for breath. Couldn't he see? "I'm not." She gripped her stomach as it threatened to lurch again. "Not all right. Nothing is all right." She panted, trying to catch her breath and settle her shuddering stomach.

"Shh." Kirk's head bent suddenly close as he soothed her. "Deep breaths. Don't gulp air. You'll only make it worse."

She shoved him away and took a step back. "How can I make it worse?" Her voice rose as she looked up at him. "How can I *possibly* make it worse?"

But rather than give her the space she desired, he stepped closer this time, his voice low, his hazel eyes flicking to the skyline and back to her. "Keep your voice down. If you get caught, I guarantee things will get worse in a hurry."

Fear shot through her sorrow, deflating it somewhat. "Caught?"

A patient look settled across his features as he worked with the sails. "The rebels behind the attack this evening." He spoke so quietly, she found she had to step closer just to hear him. "You don't think they'll be content to just scare you off, do you? That wasn't a demonstration by an unhappy fringe group, in case you were wondering. No, that was a coordinated attempt, and I fear they may have the military on their side."

His words were in plain English, the official language of Lydia, yet she couldn't make sense of what he was saying. As Kirk untied the line that held a sail, Anastasia followed him. "The explosions?" She ducked as he swung a jib around past her, then stepped closer again as he used it to catch the breeze. "You think the military attacked the royal motorcade?"

Kirk remained silent as he tied a complicated knot that held the rope taut.

"My father is the head of the military." She tried to sort out what had happened, as though it was a game of hide-and-seek like they'd played as children, and if she could just solve the riddle, her family would reappear. "You said you'd heard rumors. An uprising?" She followed him back as he unlocked the rudder, aligning the small boat with their altered course. "Kirk—talk to me. What do you know?"

"Nothing for certain." He took the steps down to the cabin and ducked out of sight.

Infuriating. The silent man would yield no more answers today than he had six years before when she'd asked him about her brother. She followed him below, but rather than answer her question, he stepped past her and went back on deck, still busy sailing the boat.

"Kirk!" She followed him back into the open air.

"Shh!" This time his face bent so close to hers their foreheads nearly touched. "I told you to keep your voice down."

Stasi glanced around at the open sea. Yes, there were boats in the area, but they were far enough away and none of them seemed to be paying them any extra attention, and it was unlikely they'd be able to hear her unless they were listening closely.

But what if they were listening closely?

Chastened, she gripped her stomach before it could spasm again. "Kirk, please." Her voice trembled slightly, but she didn't care. "I don't understand what happened. My family—" She gulped a breath, her words cutting in and out in a high squeak of emotion. "I don't know what happened to my family. I don't know where we're going or who's after me." Tears flowed freely at the thought of her family members being injured or killed. "I don't even know if I can trust you."

"You can trust me. Have I ever hurt you before?"

"You took my brother away."

"I didn't take him away. He left. I simply kept my promise not to tell anyone where he went."

"So Thaddeus is alive?"

"He was last I checked."

Stasi nodded, though Kirk's words did little to reassure her. She'd never understood why her brother would go away and not give them any proof of his survival. Another sorrowful spasm racked her stomach, and she moaned.

"Here." Kirk extended a silver-wrapped piece of gum toward her. "Peppermint. To settle your stomach."

"Thank you." Stasi doubted the little stick of gum could overcome the unsettling effects of all she'd witnessed, but she appreciated his gesture. She popped the gum into her mouth, thinking if Thaddeus really was alive, she wasn't completely alone.

Kirk altered the course of the boat again, weaving them in between small islands. "You can trust me. I didn't betray your brother, not even during his murder trial. And I won't betray you."

"What does that mean?" She held his arm, a thick, strong one, feeling his muscles flex as he worked the ropes of his one-man sailboat. "You didn't betray my brother?"

The chameleon color of his hazel eyes picked up the bloodred of the sunset, its deadly hue an ill portent that stained his words. "I promised your brother that I would keep his whereabouts a secret from everyone."

"Thad *wanted* you to hide him?"

"Yes." Kirk turned his back to her, busy with the tasks of sailing the craft in a zigzagging pattern through the islands. Stasi studied his back, for the first time considering her brother's disappearance from this new angle he'd shown her.

Perhaps Kirk was a man of integrity after all. Perhaps he was actually the bravest, most honorable person through that whole messy trial. He'd taken the stand and insisted that Thaddeus wasn't dead, but to every demand for proof, he simply responded, "I can't tell you."

It had driven her father nearly mad. She'd been present for much of it, furious with Kirk through almost all of it, but at the same time, she'd sensed there was something more to the story just below the surface, if only Kirk would break his infuriating silence.

The man seemed determined never to tell more than was absolutely necessary. But she needed answers, now more than ever. "Where are we headed?"

"Dorsi."

Stasi startled. "But it's forbidden. It's dangerous."

"Not as dangerous as what's behind us."

She absorbed his words. He had a decent point there. "But—"

"It's the last place anyone will come to look for us. Everyone knows to visit the Island of Dorsi is to take your life into your own hands."

"And for good reason. No one has ever visited Dorsi and returned alive."

"I have."

Stasi stepped back with the sway of the boat and shook her head slowly. "Travel to the Island of Dorsi has been banned for nearly a century. The walls are crumbling away and there are land mines everywhere."

"For the record—" Kirk's face bore a smile that was just enough of a smirk to irritate her "—I've been visiting Dorsi for over a decade and never witnessed a crumbling wall or any falling rocks that I did not personally dislodge. And as far as I can tell there is no substance behind the rumor about the land mines. I suspect your grandfather's government didn't want to deal with the liability of tourists visiting the island. If they came in droves, they really could start the walls crumbling. The land mine story was likely invented to keep people away."

The smirk had faded from his lips, replaced by a serious expression. "For our sakes—" his tone grew solemn "—I'm quite glad they did. Now, I've got to bring the boat in, and it's tricky enough in full daylight, so in this darkness you'll have to excuse me."

While Kirk focused on steering the boat toward the island, which loomed ominously above the water in the waning light of the setting sun, Stasi stood back and tried to absorb all he'd told her.

He'd been visiting the island for over a decade? She couldn't imagine why anyone would want to visit the dangerous place, let alone return there. As she watched, the boat pulled closer through the lapping waves. Kirk guided the craft past jagged rocks and the signs warning them in various languages and morbid pictographs just what might happen if one ventured too close.

She shuddered as the rocks slid by. It seemed likely they would hit one, but Kirk's steady hands never faltered, and the boat slid past rock after rock. The sun spilled its dying light over the sea, and in its red glow Stasi spotted the narrow inlet Kirk had pointed them toward.

To her amazement, the nimble sailboat slipped into the

restricted space, past rocky cliffs that protected a secret cove, traveling around a bend to where a soft, sandy beach stretched out behind the rocky promontory, beyond the sight of anyone traveling past the island.

"How did you know this was here?" She followed Kirk as far as the rail. Then Kirk hopped out of the boat with a rope, splashing through the shallow water and pulling the prow onto the sand before securing the rope tightly around a large jutting rock.

"Thad was always curious about the place. He found a book in the king's library that had a map. It was a few centuries old, so we didn't know if any of this would still exist. But obviously, it does." He stood beside the boat and reached his arms out toward her.

Stasi hesitated. She knew he was only offering to help her down, and she appreciated his thoughtfulness, but she was wary of having contact with the man she'd spent so long despising. In spite of his reassurances, she still wasn't certain he was someone she wanted to trust.

But she also didn't want to stay on the boat alone, so she jumped down and his hands caught her about the waist, settling her effortlessly on her bare feet on the dry sand, just beyond the lapping water.

He held her just long enough for her to gain steady footing, but she still felt herself flush from the contact. She knew he was only being polite, but he'd always been a handsome man who'd somehow grown more attractive while she'd been ignoring him.

"Are you all right?" he whispered before he let her go.

She looked into his face, but with the high rocky walls blocking the low sun, she could make out neither honor nor deceit in his expression. "Fine." Her legs felt rubbery after the dipping boat ride. When she tried to take a step back, away from him, her knees dipped and she wobbled, flinging her arms wide in an attempt to catch herself.

"Your Highness!" Kirk's strong hands steadied her waist, keeping her upright, while she overcorrected her careening dip and smashed back into his chest. "Careful, now." The words rumbled below her ear.

She caught a note of something in the undercurrent of his comforting words, and she kept her cheek pressed against him as she tried to think what it was. In contrast to the fear and grief she'd felt all evening, Kirk's undertone carried something like warmth or affection, maybe even longing.

Longing?

No, that couldn't be it. "I'm fine now." She pulled away from him and stood on her own two feet.

"This way." He turned and took off up a curving path as though in a hurry to leave their close brush behind.

Still barefoot after having removed her high heels on the boat, Stasi picked her way up the soft sand after him. By the time the sandy path blended into rocks, Kirk was far ahead of her.

The rocks felt sharp against her unaccustomed feet, and though she lifted her long skirt up to her knees, she could hardly see anything of the path in the darkness. Trying to gauge how much farther she had to go, she looked ahead just in time to see Kirk disappear around a bend in the path.

Loneliness washed its heavy hand over her, and she bowed under its weight. Uncertain whether or not the reverberations of her voice would send rocks crashing down, she called out quietly, "Kirk?"

The silence felt a little too hollow and the darkness too deeply shadowed in this forgotten place where the cliffs blocked the setting sun. The fear and grief she'd been battling all evening began to get the upper hand again, and she tried to sniff back her tears.

Then Kirk leaped back into sight in front of her. "Yes?"

Her sense of relief at his reappearance surprised her with its intensity. Had she been that afraid of being alone? Or was she simply that glad to see him again? She fumbled for words. "My feet." She pointed her naked toes toward him. "The rocks—"

Without another word he scooped her into his arms, cradling her like an infant in her evening gown, and clambered up the path, carrying her as though she didn't weigh a thing.

She tried not to think too much about how being in his arms made her feel, but there was that warmth she'd felt a moment ago. Kirk was so strong and capable—one of the strongest members of the royal guard, with a promising future ahead of him before he'd tarnished his reputation with a murder trial.

Still, he was winsome and charismatic. It would be all too easy to trust him. And after everything that had happened, she knew she was emotionally vulnerable. Surely the sudden yearning she felt to place her head on his shoulder had nothing to do with any real feelings between them. It was merely a result of the monumentally trying events of the evening.

Kirk traveled easily up the path, and moments later a limestone tower loomed ahead, cast in a golden glow by the light of the sinking sun. Without hesitating, Kirk swept her over the threshold, through an arched doorway into a wide stone room.

# THREE

The last of the sunlight blocked by four walls and a ceiling, Stasi blinked against the darkness and tightened her grip on Kirk's shoulders. "Where are we?"

"Through here is the queen's chamber. Thad and I found it all on the map. There are stairs up to the tower—it's got a glorious view all the way to Sardis. But right now I'm taking you to where Thaddeus stayed."

At the mention of her brother's name, Stasi was reminded of all the unanswered questions regarding his disappearance. "When did Thad stay here?"

"Six years ago." Kirk carried her into a smaller room and stopped.

"Before he—?" She let the question linger, unsure how to phrase what had happened.

Kirk settled her onto a stone bench before turning his back to her. "Before he left, yes. He was actually situated here until shortly before the trial. At that point we decided it would be best if he stayed far enough away that, no matter what they did to me, he wouldn't be tempted to return." Kirk fumbled with something in the darkness, and a moment later Stasi saw the light of a small flame in his hands.

When he turned back toward her, his face was lit by the warm glow of a candle. "This room isn't visible from the sea, so you're safe to use a light in here. But we don't want anyone to see the light and come investigate, so don't take any flame with you if you decide to explore further."

Stasi had little interest in exploring the spooky ruins, but she was eager to hear more about her brother. "Why was it so important that he not return?"

To her surprise, Kirk brought the candle over to the stone bench and sat down beside her. The glow of that tiny fire enveloped them in a small circle of light, and Stasi had to fight the urge to lean closer to him. She watched his face carefully as he spoke.

"Your brother doesn't want to be found. He and your parents had a disagreement."

Stasi tried to accept what Kirk told her, but it didn't make any sense. "I disagree with my parents all the time. I don't hide from everyone I love because of it."

Kirk leaned back against the stone wall behind them and closed his eyes. In the flickering light of the candle his face looked older than his almost-thirty years, and weary. "It's his story to tell. I can't share it with you any more than I could have told anyone else."

She placed a tentative hand on his arm. "But everyone thinks you killed him. If he's not dead, why doesn't he show his face to prove them all wrong?" She couldn't stand that Kirk had been willing to let her believe he was a murderer all this time if he really wasn't.

With a sigh, Kirk opened his eyes and looked at her directly. "If your father knew where your brother was, he'd do everything in his power to bring him back. Thad couldn't risk that. I've told everyone as much of the truth as he wanted me to tell. The rest I promised to keep secret. From everyone, including you."

Stasi struggled to absorb the news. Granted, Thaddeus was the oldest and she the youngest child in their family, so in spite of being close to her siblings, there had always been that seven-year distance between them. She'd been only seventeen when he'd disappeared, and she'd taken the news very hard—not only the loss of her brother, but the loss of Kirk as a dear family friend.

She wanted very much to believe Thad was still alive, and that Kirk hadn't ever done anything to hurt him. But she had to steel herself against one inescapable reality: Kirk was keeping secrets from her. However well intentioned those secrets might be, the simple fact was he hadn't told her the whole truth. Beyond his obscure reassurances, she knew nothing of what had become of her brother. Until the gaps in his story were filled, she didn't dare trust Kirk. Not completely.

Hoping to push Kirk to reveal her brother's whereabouts, she met his eyes. "If the rest of my family was killed in today's ambush, Thaddeus may be the only living relative I have left."

Kirk bowed his head over the candle. When he looked her in the face again, she was surprised to see wetness twinkling in his eyes. His voice was rough when he spoke. "If I learn that the rest of your family has been killed, I will take you to him."

She felt a spiral of fear swirl through her stomach. If Kirk had killed her brother, then his words indicated he would kill her, too. But everything about him, from the pain on his face to the way he'd protected her that day, indicated he had only the purest of intentions. Her heart rammed inside her chest, still reeling from the many shocks of the evening, wavering furiously between believing one reality or the other.

Kirk stood. "Thaddeus had a sleeping bag here, as well as some stores of food."

"Food that was left here six years ago?" Stasi rose to stand beside him.

"Canned food stays good for a long time. You should be able to find something edible. There are wild strawberries on the north side of the island, and excellent fishing in the inlet. Your brother's fishing pole was in the box where I found this candle. And there's a freshwater well in the courtyard."

The way he spoke made it sound as though she'd be on her own to fend for herself—possibly for some time. "Where are you going to be?"

"I'm going back to the mainland."

"You're going to leave me?" She didn't want to be abandoned on the treacherous island.

"We've got to learn what happened to your family. I can't do that from here."

"But isn't it dangerous? Surely people saw you leave the palace with me. If they're looking for me, they'll come after you."

The grin Kirk returned her was unsettlingly confident. "If I'm the only one who knows where you are, then I'll be the safest man in Sardis. Anyone who's looking for you won't dare kill me. That would sever their last link to you."

The meaning of his words sank in. "Is that why my parents declared you untouchable? They believe you know where Thad is?"

"Your father knows why Thad left." Kirk sighed. "He never honestly thought I killed him. The entire trial was his attempt to compel me to betray your brother—to reveal where he was hiding, or possibly to force your brother to come out of hiding to save me. The king has kept me on in the royal guard in part so he can keep an eye on me. He hates me for not telling him where Thad is."

Stasi felt alarmed by Kirk's words. Though they seemed to explain parts of her brother's case that had always bothered her, in some ways, they raised more questions than they answered. "I don't understand. Why would you go on trial and endure my father's hatred—and the scorn of the Lydian people—if you didn't have to?"

"But I *did* have to."

"Thaddeus could have returned."

"No, Stasi, he couldn't. I'm sorry I can't share more details. What your father did—" Kirk's voice grew rough, and his Adam's apple bobbed up and down, betraying emotion. "It was bad, Stasi. Bad enough for Thaddeus to go away forever."

Much as she couldn't fathom her father doing anything that wasn't pure, noble, right and blameless, Kirk's statements had the reinforcement of six years' history to back them up. A chill of fear prickled goose bumps down her arms. "Do you think it has anything to do with today's attack?"

Kirk froze, and Stasi thought she spotted a glimmer of fear in his usually fearless eyes. "If it does—" he swallowed, and seemed to need a few breaths before he could continue "—then God help us."

Stasi didn't understand all that was going on—Kirk was still withholding information—but she knew enough to know that whatever they were up against, Kirk was scared of it. He'd once stared down a murder trial without blinking. If Kirk was afraid, then she had reason to be afraid, too.

And it also occurred to her that she'd hated and avoided him for six years, when perhaps he'd been acting in a nobler manner than the king. Moved by the thought of what Kirk had been through on her brother's behalf, Stasi reached for his arm. "I'm sorry."

He looked down at her, and suddenly she realized how close they were standing, and how strong the arm under her hand felt, and how much she'd missed spending time with him.

"Don't be." He leaned a little closer. "I took a vow to protect your family when I joined the royal guard. That meant standing by your brother when his own father tried to betray him. That means doing whatever I can to keep you safe."

Stasi considered the face so close to hers, his eyes so familiar to the laughing boy she'd known throughout her childhood. Freckles she'd all but forgotten now reappeared like old friends, but on a face matured by time and trials. Had her father really done something so awful her brother saw no other option but to run away? She hated to think it was true. And yet, she'd seen the shadows that had haunted her father's eyes since the time her brother had disappeared. What had King Philip done? And why?

Whatever it was, Kirk had stood by her brother, and now he'd kept her from danger, too. "You went beyond the call of duty. I wouldn't ask you to do that for me."

"It's not up to you." He stood, and her hand fell away from his arm. "I need to be going."

"Must you?" Stasi blushed when she heard her impulsive words. She only meant that she didn't want to be left alone on the island, especially if he was taking the only boat for an undetermined period of time. She'd be stuck, practically marooned.

A smile flickered at the corner of his mouth. "I promise to return quickly."

"What if you can't?"

He tipped his head thoughtfully, as though her words had prompted him for the first time to consider that he wasn't immortal. For some time he stood still, apparently mulling over a decision.

Stasi studied his handsome face, his sandy-brown hair and the broad sweep of his shoulders. As a child she'd absolutely adored him. For the last six years, she'd hated him.

His deep voice sounded reluctant when he finally spoke. "You make an excellent point. It would be irresponsible for me to leave you here without anyone to protect you, but I can't take you with me. And yet, there isn't anyone in the royal guard or in the military who I know for certain we can trust. Not under the circumstances."

"Then what?"

Finally, Kirk made a resigned face and pulled out his phone. "Ah, good. The cell phone towers in Sardis still cover this island. I'm going to call Thad." Kirk's eyes hardened, his expression fiercely solemn. "We must keep the conversation brief. We have no guarantees that this line is secure. Your brother already knows the rules. Everyone has a code name. You must not say anything that would give away who you are, where you are, or who he is. It would endanger you both. Understand?"

The fear she'd felt throughout the evening was crystallized in his request. She'd seen the explosions. She understood the danger of the situation, even if she didn't know who was behind the attacks or why they'd occurred. "I promise."

Kirk nodded, then dialed and held the phone to his ear.

"Thank God you called. I've been worried sick." The voice that carried through the phone was just loud enough for Stasi to make out the words. "I've seen the news. Tell me they're not all dead."

"Not all. I've got Juliet with me right now."

"Praise the Lord."

Stasi's skin prickled with goose bumps at the sound of her brother's voice, and she stepped closer to Kirk, straining to hear more of the voice she'd long thought she might never hear again.

"Keep her safe," the distant voice insisted. "What about everyone else?"

"I don't know," Kirk answered. "I've got her holed up in your old hiding place. I'm heading back to town to learn what I can. I hope to have good news for you."

"Bless you."

Kirk looked thoughtful as he spoke. "If you don't hear from me in three days, send someone for Juliet. Don't come yourself."

There was a pause. "It's that bad, then?"

"I'll do everything I can, but I don't know what we're up against. I can't leave her here indefinitely."

Stasi suspected he might be close to ending the call. She reached for the phone, eager to speak with her brother.

"Juliet wants to talk to you." Kirk handed over the phone, warning her, "Remember."

She nodded solemnly and held the phone to her ear before realizing she didn't know what to say, especially if she wasn't to give away her brother's identity. "Are you—" She swallowed back the rest of her question.

"I am."

It was her brother's voice. Her heart leaped inside of her.

"Don't give my friend any trouble." Thaddeus didn't use Kirk's name. Then, as though he suspected she might have her doubts, Thad assured her, "You can trust him completely. Right now, he might be the only person you can trust."

"What's going on?" Stasi asked, knowing that if her brother had heard a report on the news, he might have more information than they did.

"All I know is that there's been an uprising. No one has claimed responsibility as of yet."

Stasi hesitated. There was so much she wanted to ask him, but she wasn't sure what she could say without giving away important details if their conversation wasn't private.

"Take care. I love you."

"I love you, too." Stasi couldn't fight back her tears. She handed the closed phone back to Kirk with a trembling hand.

Kirk lifted the lid on another of the compartments that blended in seamlessly with the stone walls—secret enclosures she wouldn't have guessed were there had she not watched him open them. He fished out a sleeping bag and handed her the candle.

"I need to get going. Try to get some rest. I'll be back for you as soon as I'm able." He pressed the phone into her other hand, closing her trembling fingers securely over it. "I can't allow this to fall into the wrong hands now that I've used it to call your brother. But please, don't use it unless there's an emergency. If I'm not back in three days, your brother will send someone for you."

Fear whipped up a froth of questions in her mind. "But how will I know—"

"Just trust me." The tips of his fingers hovered an inch from her lips, silencing her questions without touching her royal mouth. "I have no intention of being gone more than a few hours, but it would be irresponsible of me not to provide a backup plan given the circumstances."

Kirk bent his head close to hers in the flickering candlelight. "I just don't want you to worry." He took a step back and spread his arms wide. "Enjoy this beautiful island. Your brother loved this place. Your ancestors did, too."

He looked down at her.

She tried to raise a smile to her lips, but sorrow and fear wouldn't let her. "My code name is Juliet?" There were too many details for her to keep track of them all, but she figured that one might be important if she had to contact her brother again. "What is Thad's code name?"

"Regis."

"And yours?"

Kirk turned his back to her, pulling a pillow from the storage space that had looked so much like the rest of the stone wall before he'd lifted its secret lid. "You don't need to know mine."

"But what if—"

He gently tipped up her chin with the tips of his fingers. "It will all come out all right."

Looking into his eyes, which were earnest and sincere, Stasi wished she could believe him. "How do you know?"

"God is in charge. And God is good."

She took a shaky breath. "How could God let a thing like this happen?"

"Your Highness—" He spoke her title slowly, sweetly. She liked the sound of it on his lips. "It is night now, but the sun will shine again. Have faith." He dropped her chin and walked away through the darkness.

As she watched him go, she clutched her little candle. Her heart twisted out a desperate prayer that everything would come out all right, somehow—though she couldn't imagine how.

The moon was high when Kirk docked his boat and resolutely stepped onto the pier. He'd formed a plan in his mind as he'd sailed into Sardis, and now he headed for his parents' place, a small cottage behind the palace. Albert and Theresa Covington both held high positions in the royal household. If there was any news, they would know it. And he needed them to see that he was all right. After all that had happened, he knew they would be worrying.

He carried his duffel bag back to the Jeep, which was parked, undisturbed, where he'd left it. A good sign. It meant that, however coordinated the attack on the royal family might have been, whoever was behind it had not yet gotten around to making an organized search for the Jeep. That much made sense. They'd probably have much more urgent priorities.

The sound of the lapping sea faded as Kirk started the vehicle. It was after midnight and no one appeared to be anywhere around. Kirk drove toward the palace and parked along a side street a couple of blocks away, pulling out his personal items from where he'd stashed them, tossing them into the duffel bag, then walking the rest of the distance.

Skirting the rear gate of the royal grounds, Kirk decided to scale the wall instead of using his thumbprint to gain entry. Granted, the print would be easier, but his entrance would be recorded in the security computer. He couldn't risk giving away his location—not with the likelihood that someone might soon get around to looking for him.

Fortunately, he'd had plenty of practice scaling the castle walls with Thaddeus when they were growing up. He made it over without any trouble and found his way to the cottage.

There was still a light on in the kitchen. Kirk tried the door and found it locked, but he knocked and his mother answered, pulling him into a tight hug, and then, a moment later, shaking him by his shoulders.

"They said you'd been killed at the marina," Theresa Covington accused her son.

His father, Albert, rose from his seat at the table. "Folks saw you driving Princess Stasi in a Jeep. It was on the news. There's a rumor that the two of you were killed and your bodies thrown into the sea."

"Did you believe it?" Kirk asked, looking back and forth from one parent to the other. He wasn't at all surprised that someone might report him dead, and Princess Stasi killed, too. But he thought his parents had more faith in him than to believe such an obviously false report.

"We don't know what to believe." His mother wore a wary expression. "They're reporting the whole royal family has been killed in an ambush."

"And yet—" his father leaned in and spoke quietly "—from what I've heard, there aren't any bodies—not that fit the royal family, anyway. Two drivers and a guard were killed in the blasts. I knew all three of them." As the longtime head butler and estate manager at the palace, Kirk's father knew everyone who worked there—even those who worked outside of the main castle.

Kirk felt the sting of loss that innocent people had died. But at the same time, his father's words buoyed his hope. If the bodies of the royal family hadn't been found, then they still were alive. Somewhere. "Stasi will be glad to hear it."

"She's alive, then?" Theresa Covington finally let go of her son's shoulders.

"Alive and safe, for now," Kirk assured them both. "I don't know who barricaded her in her room, but thank God they did—that's why she missed her ride in the limousine. She was with me in the Jeep when the first blast hit. But that's where the truth of that rumor ends. I got her out of Sardis as quickly as I could."

"But now what will you do?" his father asked.

"I was hoping to learn what's happened to the rest of her family—she's desperate for news of them. I'd like to believe they've survived. If we can locate any of them, I'll take Stasi to them. Otherwise, I'll take her to Thaddeus. In the meantime, though, I may have to hide her. I'll need supplies."

His parents tensed when he mentioned the name of the presumed-dead heir to the Lydian throne. Though Kirk had assured them long ago that Thaddeus was alive and well, he knew they, like the rest of the Lydian population, still sometimes wondered if he hadn't possibly committed the crime he'd been accused of. His folks had stood by him, but he hadn't given them any more reason to believe him than he'd granted anyone else. He'd promised Thad. And he was a man of his word.

Kirk had many questions for his parents. "Who was behind the attacks? And what do they want?"

"I've not heard a motive, and no one has claimed responsibility yet." Albert pointed to a small television set in the corner of the kitchen that was broadcasting news updates with the volume turned low. "I don't know what will happen, or what will become of the Royal House of Lydia."

"What about the two of you? Headed back to the U.S.?" Kirk's parents were both American citizens. His mother had been best friends with Queen Elaine when they were both girls, growing up in a small town near Atlanta, Georgia. When Elaine had married then-Prince Philip, Albert and Theresa had come to Lydia to work for her. They'd remained close friends with the royal family, and Theresa was still best friends with Queen Elaine. But given the circumstances and their known allegiance to the royal family, they would likely be safer back in America.

At his suggestion, his parents exchanged worried looks.

"We've talked about it," Albert admitted.

But Theresa shook her head. "There's no threat to our lives. As long as the royal family remains unaccounted for, I feel we have to stay. What if one of them tries to contact us? I came to Lydia to help my best friend. I can't run out on her in her time of need."

Kirk appreciated his parents' devotion. He felt the same way. "Still, I think you should keep a low profile. Everyone knows how close you are to the king and queen."

"Many people are loyal to the king and queen. If the insurgents go after all of them, there will be no one left in Lydia," Albert predicted.

"Good point." Kirk appreciated his father's attitude. He stood and paced the room nervously. Much as he would have loved to learn more about what was going on, he'd promised Stasi he'd be back. And no one else knew where she was. If anything happened to him, she'd be on her own.

"I should get back to Stasi. We'll need food for a few days. And, Mother—" he looked up at the woman who, as the household manager for the entire palace, had access to nearly every room in the castle "—I don't suppose there would be any way you could discreetly pack a bag for Stasi? Some of her own clothes and shoes? She's in an evening gown right now."

Theresa's eyes twinkled. "I always keep bags packed and waiting for every member of the royal family—for various occasions and seasons, no less. Give me five minutes."

While she was gone, Kirk and his father put together a bag of food supplies, a radio and plenty of batteries. Kirk was familiar with what Thad had left stowed on the island, which left more room for essentials.

"You'll want this." Albert handed him a first-aid kit.

"We've got Thad's."

"And it's six years old." Albert shoved the first-aid kit into Kirk's hands. "This one is fresh."

When Kirk reached for the kit, his father hesitated before handing it over. "You're alone with the princess?"

Kirk immediately knew what his father was thinking. The princess was far out of his league. She was to be given white-gloved treatment, always. He'd had lectures about it all the time as a child, especially as Stasi had blossomed into a lovely young woman. "She's safe in my care," he reassured his father, "from *any* threat."

"She's royal. You're not." His father handed him the kit with warning in his voice. "Never forget that."

By the time Kirk had the bag ready, his mother was back. "There's an unnatural amount of commotion over there, especially when you consider no one's home."

"Did you learn anything new?" Kirk asked.

Theresa shook her head adamantly. "I got out of there in a hurry. Didn't like the feel of it. You've got to be *careful*." His mother handed over the bag. "You don't know what you're up against. Things might not go the way you want them to."

Kirk backed away toward the door, giving each of his parents a hug on his way out. "Lydia is a Christian nation," he reminded them. "God will watch over us."

"Depending on who has risen to power," his father warned him, "Lydia may not be a Christian nation anymore."

# FOUR

Darkness. As long as Kirk kept his head down, he prayed the darkness would be enough to keep him disguised. He tossed the bags over the wall and followed them a second later. Much as he would have loved to learn more about what was afoot, too many people didn't like him, and the situation was too volatile. He needed to get back to Stasi.

Leaving the vehicle behind, Kirk opted for the flexibility and stealth of traveling by foot to where he'd left his boat at the marina. The warm June night was deceptively lovely.

To his relief, Kirk didn't see any unusual activity as he approached the marina. His boat bobbed exactly where he'd left it. Kirk climbed aboard and prepared to push off.

"*Where* was she seen?"

The question floated on the air from somewhere nearby, the words almost too faint to pick up in their entirety. Kirk's hands stilled on the knot he'd been untying, and his ears pricked up for more.

The voices grew clearer as two figures drew closer. "At the United States Embassy. According to Sergio, she stepped inside with her bodyguard. They were in and out so fast, the security camera didn't pick up a decent image of either of them."

"Is that the same bodyguard she asked to have removed?"

Tense laughter. "I think so."

"I wonder what's up."

Kirk had been wondering as much, himself, and then some. Who were they talking about? Possibly Stasi's mother or sister? He'd heard something about Princess Isabelle asking to have her bodyguard removed earlier in the week.

The two men had walked down the pier, and now stood silently just out of sight. Kirk wanted to know more. Who were the men who were talking? Had another member of the royal family survived?

It would make all the difference in the world to Stasi if he could bring her good news. He'd left her looking so forlorn. She'd be thrilled to hear someone had spotted her sister since the attacks—if that was, indeed, what the men had been discussing. But Kirk didn't want to bring Stasi news that her sister might be alive, only to have her hopes dashed a second time if he'd assumed wrong.

Kirk weighed his options. Should he try to talk to the men and learn more? Or should he head back to Stasi straightaway? It didn't seem likely that talking to the men would lead to trouble, but then, Kirk had learned otherwise the hard way before.

Kirk had been a member of the royal guard ever since he and Thaddeus had completed their training with the Lydian military at twenty-one. He'd never gotten along perfectly with all of his coworkers, first because he was best friends with the prince, and then because he'd been accused of killing him.

Following Thad's disappearance, Kirk had become a polarizing figure. Some saw him as a rebel and an inspiration. Others believed he was a traitor. Some were suspicious of him, and others jealous or annoyed by all the attention he received from the media. Many, he knew, were watching him, waiting for him to slip up and give away new evidence that would prove he'd killed Thaddeus.

Would the men on the pier talk to him? Or would he only be giving himself away?

Kirk prayed silently, his hands folded over the knot he'd been working on. *Lord, what should I do?*

The two men had reached the end of the pier, and now their footfalls indicated they were headed back his way. Kirk stepped back into a shadow and watched the men as they passed by.

He knew them! They were members of the royal guard—Jason and Linus, two men who'd always seemed to get along well enough with him, even after Thad's disappearance. The pair continued down toward the boardwalk, and were nearly out of sight again. Kirk leaped back up onto the dock and hurried after them, clearing his throat to let them know he was approaching.

The men spun around, clearly on their guard.

"Jason, Linus." Kirk held up his hands in an innocent gesture. "Good to see you two."

"Kirk?" Linus was clearly surprised to see him. "I heard you were dead."

Before Kirk could explain, Jason grabbed his arm. "You might want to get out of here."

"Why? What—"

Jason cut him off. "We arranged to meet a couple of members of the royal guard. I'm hoping to learn more about what's been happening." He shook his head, as though there were more to explain, but no time for it. "Word is, Viktor Bosch is looking for you. You were seen leaving the palace with Anastasia. There's a price on your head."

Even as he spoke, headlights swept across the marina. Kirk froze. Bosch was the head of the royal guard. When Kirk had been reinstated to his position, Bosch had been furious.

Linus gave them both a grim look. "That's our boys."

The car stopped with its headlights trained on Kirk's face, and the doors flew open.

About to run toward his boat, Kirk was stopped by Jason's grip on his arm. "Not that way. They'll have recognized you already."

Kirk glanced around the marina. Jason was right. If he ran toward his boat, they might follow him, or guess he'd taken the princess out to sea. From there, it would be only a matter of time until they checked Dorsi. No, heading that direction didn't seem wise.

"I'm off then. Nice chatting with you." He threw a deliberately casual wave over his shoulder and pointed his face away from the approaching figures, taking off at a relaxed stride down the boardwalk.

"You, there."

Kirk pretended not to hear. What choice did he have? It was that or run, and if there was a price on his head, running would only invite more trouble.

An overhead light illumined far more of his path than he wanted.

"Covington!"

A spur of pier bisected the boardwalk. Kirk turned down that way, picking up his pace, hoping to reach the shadows of the yachts farther down the dock. Two royal guard Jet Skis bobbed in the water at the end of the pier, next to a royal guard motorboat. The royal guard had always maintained a coast guard element, a remnant from the centuries before when the royal family had lived on Dorsi.

If he could just reach the watercrafts, Kirk hoped he might be able to get away.

Boots pounded down the hollow boardwalk behind him.

"Covington!"

They were closing in on him. Kirk sprinted down the pier, but the Jet Skis were still fifty meters away, and his options were few. He'd left his boat down a different pier. And heading out to sea might point his pursuers toward Stasi. Should he even try it?

He could hear the men breathing just behind him. Fingers swiped at the back of his shirt.

He was never going to reach the Jet Skis—wasn't even sure he wanted to. He spun to the side. There was nothing left but the Mediterranean. Kirk dived into the open water.

When the moon rose high in the sky, Anastasia climbed the queen's tower and found the view, as Kirk had promised, to be breathtaking. She could see the glittering lights of Sardis far in the distance, and said a prayer for the safety of her family.

Had Kirk arrived safely in Sardis? She wondered if he was there now. At the thought of him her heart began to beat rapidly.

For the last six years she had hated him, refused to speak to him, walked away whenever he entered a room. She'd felt he'd betrayed the trust of her family by murdering her brother.

But her brother was not dead. In fact, it occurred to her, in being far away from Sardis when the attack took place, Thad's life had been spared.

So Stasi had Kirk to thank for both their lives.

She looked down from the other window of the tower into the former castle yard. Much more remained of the stone structure than she'd imagined. It had once been a formidable fortress, and was still an architectural masterpiece of great beauty, stonework jutting up from solid rock as though it had grown there. On the far side of the tower battlement, the castle overlooked cliffs that fell way into deep darkness. Far, far below, she could hear the steady wash of waves against the rocks.

No wonder Thaddeus had loved it there. Their ancestors had done an amazing job building the castle during the early centuries of Lydia's history. Though she understood that the castle had become roughly inaccessible as storms washed away the stretch of land that had once connected it to the mainland, she still felt a pang of regret that it had ever been abandoned.

But then, if the fortress on Dorsi had never been abandoned, she would not have had a place to hide. So perhaps, she realized, she ought to be grateful that no one ever visited the place.

She said her morning prayers as the sun rose, its gentle pink streaks coloring the Mediterranean with the promise of a lovely day. She resolved to *try* to enjoy the island, as Kirk had suggested. In a way, it reminded her of her childhood exploits with Kirk and her siblings, exploring the expansive palace grounds.

Back then they'd only pretended to have such an adventure. Now she was living it, but she'd gladly give it up in exchange for seeing everyone alive again.

As the sun began to creep higher in the sky, Stasi wondered if Kirk's absence was a bad sign. She tried to tell herself that he must have discovered so much that he was trying to uncover the whole plot against her family before coming back for her. But she knew that couldn't be it. Even if Kirk had been delayed himself, if it was safe for her to return to Sardis, he'd have sent someone for her.

No, his absence hinted that things were far worse in the capital city than she'd feared.

One other difficulty plagued her. She'd realized she owed Kirk an apology for treating him so harshly. When everyone had turned against him, she should have given him the benefit of the doubt. She'd always known him to be a man of integrity, with total loyalty to the crown. Why had she been so quick to believe the accusations against him?

Kirk tried to propel himself forward with a few strong kicks, but his clothes and shoes weighed him down. When he pulled his head up for air, the glance he stole behind him told him he hadn't made it very far.

The foreboding clatter of a boat motor chugging to life told him he might not make it much farther.

The royal guard motorboat slapped waves crossways as it fought its way toward him, its searchlight cutting through the darkness, homing in on him. As it pulled closer, Kirk gulped a breath and descended, kicking his way down into the cooler depths.

He looked up through the churning water. The blades of the outboard motor cut through the water above him. Bright light penetrated the sea, the leering faces of the men above him distorted by the water.

Wishing he could stay underwater forever, Kirk tried to swim away from the men, but it was all he could do to keep his head down. When his lungs demanded air and he pulled his head up for a quick gulp, before he could duck back down again, rough hands pulled him by his shirt collar, nearly choking him.

They threw him onto the boat. Before Kirk could get enough of a breath to think straight, a harsh voice demanded, "Hold him for me," and while two figures stilled his fighting, another man delivered several blows to his midsection.

He couldn't get a decent look at any of them. They had the bright searchlight pointed at his face.

"The princess was seen departing in your company. Where is she?" a voice demanded.

Kirk could see nothing beyond the glaring light.

"I asked you a question! Where is she?" The question was followed by a ringing blow across his jaw.

Even if he could have formed a coherent response, Kirk was determined to keep his mouth shut. The man didn't need further provocation. As fists pummeled him one after another, Kirk wondered if the men weren't intent on beating him to death.

"Bosch is on his way," one of the men reported, as his attacker sent another stinging blow across his face. "Leave the torture to him. He's wanted to get his hands on Covington for a long time. Let's bring him in."

The boat chugged back toward the dock, and one of his attackers sent another blow across Kirk's face. "And don't even think about trying to get away!"

They shoved him up on the dock, and Kirk stumbled reluctantly forward while trying to think how to escape. He needed to get back to Stasi. He knew how frightened she must be. If he didn't return, she'd be on her own. Worse yet, Thad might follow up on his request to send someone for her, which could potentially expose him to detection.

The men reached the boardwalk, and Kirk realized it might only be a matter of minutes before Viktor Bosch, the perpetually belligerent head of the royal guard, arrived. Bosch had long made his resentment toward Kirk perfectly clear. Kirk suspected the man's bitterness extended beyond having a judge order Kirk reinstated in the guard. Viktor's animosity ran deep.

Just as Kirk contemplated trying to fight off the four men who held him, a sound off to his right caught his attention. Spinning sideways, he used the distraction to his advantage, catching the man on his right in the gut with his knee before knocking him cold.

He spun back the other way. Two figures had arrived, exchanging blows with his captors. Kirk approached the remaining man, but the figure held his hands up in a gesture of surrender.

"I was only following orders."

Kirk stared at him a moment longer. He knew the man, but only by sight. It was too much to try to sort out who was on whose side, and when he nodded, the man ran off. One of his attackers staggered into him, reeling backward from a blow.

For the first time, Kirk got a good look at the two men who'd come to his aid.

Linus and Jason.

"I told you to get out of here," Jason reminded him.

A pinprick of distant headlights pierced the predawn darkness of the hillside.

"You two should go, too." Kirk tried to catch his breath, realizing for the first time that he was bleeding from a split lip.

Linus knocked his attacker cold. "We're going."

"The woman." Kirk remembered just in time. "At the embassy? I heard you talking—"

Jason and Linus were already on their way down the boardwalk, and the attacker who'd surrendered was already long gone. There was no one to overhear them. "Princess Isabelle," Linus called over his shoulder. "She's on the run."

"Thank you." Kirk sprinted back toward the dock where his boat was moored, fighting the throbbing pain that pounded up from each place he'd been struck. The headlights neared the marina, and he wouldn't have much time.

Untying his boat, he started his trolling motor and clung to the rail as stars danced across his vision. The pinch he felt with each ragged breath told him he'd cracked a rib in all the abuse he'd taken from those men.

But it told him one other thing, a far more ominous portent than the likelihood of a painful recovery. Whoever was behind the attack on the royal family meant business. And they had plenty of power on their side to enforce it.

Stasi was in trouble. He needed to get back to her—if he could get his boat to Dorsi without passing out.

Stasi watched the approaching sailboat cautiously. She'd found a pair of binoculars among the many supplies her brother had left on the island, and she trained them on the boat.

"Please be Kirk," she prayed. The boat looked enough like his, but she'd only been on it once, and that was in the dark and a good part of the time inside a duffel bag, so she certainly wasn't an expert on what it looked like.

As the little sloop edged toward the island, Stasi spotted a figure slumped over the rudder. Was it Kirk? He looked like he could hardly hold himself up.

Her heart tore. She'd been so horribly worried about him, and had finally concluded that it had been unwise for him to return to Sardis. Too bad she'd realized it too late.

When the prow dipped toward the hidden inlet, Stasi jumped down from her perch on the castle wall and clambered across the smooth rocks to meet him. She wore a T-shirt she'd found among her brother's things, and the cuffs of Thad's shorts hung past her knees, the waist folded over and tied securely with an improvised twine belt.

She reached the little strip of beach and spotted Kirk on the deck with a rope in his hands. When he tossed it to her, he looked as though he might come tumbling out after it.

"Are you all right?"

He didn't answer, but tossed down bags. The first few held food, then a bag she recognized as one of her own travel bags—one that was always kept stocked for impromptu trips. Lastly, he tossed down a first-aid kit.

A groan from Kirk caught her attention, and she looked

up in time to see him ease himself to sitting on the edge of the boat. His handsome face looked pale under his tan, and his eyes were nearly closed.

"Do you need help?" She realized he had yet to speak.

Kirk nodded and slumped forward.

"What do—" Before she could finish her question, he keeled off the side of the boat.

Stasi tried to catch him or at least break his fall, but he'd always been much bigger than she was, and rather than do much to help, she ended up flat on the sand beside him. He dropped onto his side with his face in the sand and his legs in water up to his knees.

"Kirk?" Her level of concern skyrocketed. "What's wrong?" She turned his head to the side so she could see his face, and wiped away the sand that stuck to his skin.

"Oh, Kirk!" She gasped when she saw the mass of swollen bruises and cuts that had deformed his handsome face. Suddenly realizing what the first-aid kit was for, she grabbed the supplies and set to work daubing at his cuts with cotton balls soaked with rubbing alcohol. She knew it had to sting terribly, but he didn't flinch.

"Who did this to you?" She realized she was crying only when she saw a tear splash onto his arm.

"Men working for Viktor Bosch."

"The head of the royal guard? Is he the one behind the attacks?" She winced as she realized his injuries covered more of his body. How had Kirk stayed upright long enough to make it to the island?

Resting on the ground seemed to help Kirk, because his voice grew slightly stronger. "No one has claimed responsibility. But someone has been ordering the soldiers around, and the royal guard, too."

"Who?"

"I'm sorry." Kirk drew in a ragged breath as Stasi pressed

a fresh cotton ball against a cut on his knuckle. "I don't know. I barely got out of there alive." He winced again. "That reminds me. Call Thad. Tell him not to send anyone."

"I already did."

"What?" Kirk startled.

"When you were gone so long I started to think maybe it wasn't wise for Thad to send anyone. So I called him back and told him to wait another week. He'd been watching the news, of course, but there haven't been any new developments since the attack last night and already the media has moved on."

"Maybe that's their plan."

He seemed to struggle to catch his breath, so Stasi filled in what she guessed he'd been about to say. "To wait until the world stops paying attention before they make their next move?"

"Uh-huh." His affirmation came out like a groan.

"I'm sorry if I'm hurting you. I don't want these to become infected." Stasi tried not to think about how much pain he must be in—and how much pain he'd suffered at the hands of Bosch's men.

Kirk's eyes closed.

"Are you going to be okay?"

"I'll be fine." He didn't open his eyes. "I'm thirsty."

"Let me fetch you a drink." Stasi ran to get water. She'd found the freshwater well that morning and been delighted to discover the water quality was excellent. Now she hurried back to Kirk with water in a bottle she'd found among Thad's things.

Kirk had gotten into a sitting position while she was gone, and had pulled his shirt up past his chiseled abs to his chest. He sat on the sand gingerly prodding a spot near his sternum.

"I don't think it's broken in two," he reported. "Just cracked."

"Your rib?" Stasi couldn't help gasping at the thought.

Kirk reached up for the water she offered him, but pain crossed his face as he raised his arm higher.

"Here, let me help you." She fell down on her knees in the sand in front of him and raised the water to his lips. His hand trembled as he reached for the bottle.

"It's okay. I've got it," she assured him, tipping it for him to drink. She watched him carefully, not wanting to pour more than he was ready for. Then she wiped away the drops that clung to his chin.

His weary eyes met hers, and she paused, her heart full of the many things she wanted to tell him or ask him about, but none of them seemed so important now. First and foremost, she needed to take care of his injuries.

"How did you ever manage to sail your boat in this condition?" Stasi recalled all the sail adjusting that required free use of his arms. She couldn't imagine how painful any one of those motions must have been with a cracked rib. It was obvious he'd been brutally beaten, and had clearly made it back to the island on sheer grit and determination.

"I think the adrenaline masked the pain." He took another slow sip of water. "I had to get back to you." He began to cough, and immediately winced, his shoulders bunching tight, no doubt against the increased pain his coughing fit provoked. "News." He fought to speak. "Your family. Your sister."

Stasi wasn't sure which worried her more—the thought of what had become of her family, or the pain that seemed to overcome Kirk as he tried to deliver his message.

He shook his head, almost in apology, before spitting on the sand.

Bright red blood colored the spot.

"Are you bleeding internally?" Stasi asked, her concern rising.

"It may be from the cut on my lip." Kirk took a slow breath, his eyes almost closed.

She could tell it was taking all his effort just to catch his breath without triggering another coughing fit.

"Your sister," he said slowly, his eyes still closed. "She's alive."

Stasi's squeal of happiness startled her own ears, and she had to catch herself before she threw her arms around Kirk. "Alive? Is she injured? Is she okay? Did you see her?" She bit back her questions as Kirk slowly opened his eyes.

"She was spotted at the embassy after the blast. She's on the run. I don't know much more than that."

"That is the best news." Stasi bit back her tears. "Should I try to bandage up your cuts?" She turned to the side and pulled a packet of bandages from the first-aid kit. When she faced him again, the expression on his face made her pause.

"Thank you." His hazel eyes held sincerity.

Stasi blushed. "It's the least I can do. It seems none of this would have happened if you hadn't been trying to help me. I shouldn't have let you go back to Sardis."

"I needed to go."

The strong scent of rubbing alcohol met her nostrils as she drew in a deep breath. "I'm not dreaming, am I? I was just coming to grips with the likelihood that she'd died." Giddy hope swirled in her chest. "Perhaps no one was killed, then."

His expression remained grave. "Following the attack on the motorcade, three bodies were found. Two drivers and a guard."

Stasi bit her lip and looked up at the sky. People *had* died, then. It was so awful. "There were no other bodies?"

"None."

"They're not just hiding them, covering up what they've

done?" She daubed the cotton ball as gently as she could along his bloody jaw, blowing on the spot to soothe the sting.

"It wouldn't make sense. There was even a rumor that the two of us had been tossed into the sea, but that was quickly squashed. No body, no death. It seems the members of the royal family have made an art of vanishing into the ether."

"So you believe my parents may still be alive?" As Stasi cleaned the blood from Kirk's face, she was relieved to discover much of it had come from just a few cuts.

"It's realistic to hope. And your siblings, too. We know of at least Isabelle. I can't help but hope Alexander might have made it out, too. He's a soldier. He's always been a fighter."

Stasi squeezed her eyes shut and let grateful tears flow silently down her cheeks.

The brush of Kirk's hand across her chin caught the tears before they could fall. She opened her eyes to see his face so close to hers, and gratitude welled up inside her for all he'd done. He'd whisked her away before the insurgents could find her. He'd found a safe place for her to hide and brought her good news about her family. And he'd risked so much to do so.

"Thank you," she whispered. "You deserve a medal, or possibly a statue in the park."

Kirk laughed, but there was pain behind his laughter. "I don't want a medal or a statue."

"Then what do you want?" She looked at his face as she asked the question, and watched as his eyes swept down over her.

He was tired. She knew that. The sweep of his gaze couldn't possibly mean anything more than that he was too exhausted to keep his eyes open, but she found herself blushing anyway.

His gaze fell to the bandages he'd brought. "If you could

fix up those cuts, we can lie low here for a while, until we hear it's safe to leave the island."

"Oh, yes." Stasi leaped back into action, pulling out bandages and antiseptic ointment, and tried to avoid meeting his eyes as she worked on restoring his handsome face. But her thoughts swirled, taunting her with fearful threats, from what might have become of her family, to wondering where she would go once she left the island, and how she would get there, and when.

But mostly she thought about the injured man on the sand and her increasingly complicated feelings toward him.

A distant, thumping sound prodded Kirk from sleep. He opened his eyes against the pain that seared through his ribs. Someone was beating a drum in the sky, or possibly against the dull ache in his head.

*Thrum-thrum-thrum.*

A helicopter.

Kirk snapped his eyes open and shifted his head to see the dark night sky. Where was it? Not too close, not yet, but from the sound of it, it was moving closer. Slowly. Not as though it was headed somewhere, but almost as though it was hovering. Watching.

Looking for someone.

Instinctively, Kirk began to roll to his back, to get up, but the pain that shot through him from his cracked rib put a quick stop to that. Where was he going to go, anyway? To warn the princess? And then what? If they put out to sea, they'd be spotted immediately.

Their only hope was to lie low and pray.

*Lord, hide us. Cover us, please.*

Kirk heard himself whispering the prayer, his voice weak in comparison to the steady thrum of the helicopter that grew louder, closer, bringing detection nearer with every beat of its rotors.

Light flashed across the cliff tops.

*Give Stasi the wisdom to keep her head down.*

After Stasi had bandaged him up, Kirk had fallen asleep on the sand, too weary to move. He'd awakened once before nightfall, and Stasi had insisted he eat something, but he hadn't lasted long after that. Between his injuries and the sleepless night before, he was spent.

He imagined Stasi had gone back to the queen's tower, and he could only pray she'd tried to hide any evidence of their presence on the island, but no amount of stray survival gear would be more obvious than his boat bobbing in the inlet. Years before, when he'd left Thad on the island, he and his boat had spent a minimum of time there. Thad had stayed at the island alone, and Kirk had only come and gone occasionally. When he had visited, he'd left his boat at one of the nearby islands or anchored it in the open sea before swimming out to visit his friend.

He hadn't had that option the day before. He'd been too exhausted to even move. A fatal mistake?

The light strobed, came again, dipped and flashed. They were circling the island, no doubt shining their bright lights at the shoreline, looking for any evidence that anyone had ventured near. As long as they didn't fly directly above the inlet, or over the cliff that blocked the sight of his sailboat from the open sea, there was a slight chance they might miss the signs that he and the princess were hiding out there.

The jagged turrets of the ancient fortress jutted high into the sky, as imposing a barricade now as they'd been centuries before when the castle was built. For the helicopter to fly high enough to clear them, it would be so high in the sky the party inside wouldn't be able to see much on the ground. Kirk could only pray the team in the copter would realize that, and avoid flying directly over the castle for that reason.

They didn't know about the inlet. They wouldn't know what secrets the island held.

For several long rotor-thrumming minutes, the helicopter circled the island. Then the *thrum-thrum-thrum* began to fade ever so slightly in the direction of Sardis on the mainland.

His ears strained after the sound until he could no longer tell if its echoing reverberations still beat through the distant air, or if they'd simply become so ingrained in his mind that he could hear them even though they'd faded.

"Kirk?" A feminine cry drowned out the echo of the distant sound.

Near-silent footsteps padded across the stone path until a petite set of bare feet came to rest directly in his line of sight.

"Kirk?" Stasi crouched down beside him. "Did you hear that?"

"It would have been difficult to miss." Kirk bit back the pain as he strained to sit up. At the very least he ought to look the princess in the eye while they talked. "Did they come by before—when I was away?"

"No." Distress filled her voice. "Do you think they'll come back?"

"That depends." He eased himself gingerly into a sitting position. "It may be they're just searching, with no firm idea of where we are. They know you left the palace with me right before the ambush. It's possible they may have guessed why I was at the dock last evening, and suspect you're out here, somewhere. There aren't that many places to hide off the coast of Lydia."

"They'll be back, then," Stasi pronounced. "Unless they give up looking for me."

Kirk couldn't imagine that happening, but he wasn't going

to voice his thoughts aloud. Stasi didn't need to hear another grim prognosis.

"You do still have my phone?"

"Of course," Stasi assured him. "I turned it off to save the battery."

"Smart girl. I told my father to text me if there's any news. Your sister survived the attack. She must be out there, somewhere. I'll check my messages on my phone. If Isabelle has reached safety, I'll do whatever I can to bring you to her."

Stasi scrambled away up the rocks. In a short time she was back, phone in hand.

They both waited as the little screen powered on and found its signal. It didn't escape Kirk's notice how close Stasi's forehead was to touching his as they bent over the phone, awaiting news. Kirk was more than aware, too, of the rumble of feelings he felt for the young woman beside him.

He'd always cared for her—but in an older brother protective sort of way. He'd missed her friendship when she'd stopped speaking to him six years before, but he hadn't blamed her for resenting him. Being around her again did more than revive the friendly feelings he'd once had for her. She was no longer a little girl, but a lovely young woman, and he found himself becoming more attracted to the spunky sprite. But he had no right to do so. She was a princess, and he was an accused man.

Thankfully, the screen finally illuminated, and Kirk rushed to check his messages.

Nothing. No voice mail. No texts.

He shook his head apologetically.

"Now what?"

"We wait."

"But the helicopter could return anytime."

"Or it may never return. Don't worry, I'll sort it out. You'll need your rest." Pain and weariness had already begun to overtake the alarming effects of the helicopter's shocking arrival. Kirk would need his rest, too, especially since there likely wouldn't be time for him to heal from his injuries before they had to leave the island. There simply wasn't time to spare. Each thrumming beat of the helicopter's blades had driven that point home. *We don't know what will happen tomorrow.*

# FIVE

Stasi rummaged around through the hidden storage bin that had held her brother's things, scavenging for items that might be of use to them. Her brother had left all sorts of odds and ends tucked away, many of them his own inventions.

She pulled out a crank-style flashlight and gave the handle a spin. "Is this the one Thad built from instructions he found on the internet?" When she pressed the button, the light turned on.

Kirk laughed. "He salvaged parts from a broken eggbeater, as I recall. His inventions nearly always worked." Kirk pulled out a stiff backpack that had a handle dangling from a string.

When Stasi reached for the handle, Kirk quickly moved the pack out of her reach. "Don't try it. This was Thad's emergency parachute."

"Does it work?"

"Too well. The chute ejects with too much force."

Stasi's eyes widened. "Is that how the statue on the backyard fountain lost its head?"

"I knew we'd never live that down." Kirk stashed the pack back inside the secret compartment.

A brass-hinged wooden box caught Stasi's eye. "His chess set?" Stasi reached past him and pulled the game from the bottom of the bin. "How did Thaddeus play chess alone?"

"I came out to visit him when I could." Kirk reached for the set and opened the box, which when fully opened became the playing board.

Stasi watched as Kirk set up the carved-wood pieces. "Are you planning to play?"

His eyes twinkled as he glanced up at her, then back to his task of lining up pawns in a row. "If you'll play with me. Chess is a game of military strategy. It might help us plot our next move."

"Good idea," Stasi agreed. She'd convinced Kirk to check his phone again that morning, but there were still no messages. Rather than risk running the battery down, she'd agreed they wouldn't check it again until after lunchtime. That left them with time to kill.

She settled her chin onto her hands and surveyed the board. It had been years since she'd played the game that had once been a favorite of her brother's, but she quickly warmed back up to it. Before long, she had a growing pile of Kirk's pieces.

"You just sacrificed your rook," she chastised him, claiming the piece.

"Anything to protect the king."

His words nagged at her, and she made her next move absentmindedly. "That's an important part of your life philosophy, isn't it? Protecting the king?"

"I'm a sentinel in the royal guard. It's my calling."

She looked up from the board and studied his face, which was bent in concentration over the board. She'd seen the injuries he'd sustained on her behalf. She'd seen him endure the long trial and threat of a death sentence for her brother's sake. "Chess is just a game. No one expects you to sacrifice yourself for the royal family. My life isn't worth more than yours."

He didn't answer, but moved his piece. "Checkmate."

Stasi looked down at the board.

Kirk had won. He began to clear the pieces away.

Stasi watched him, her heart trembling. She was nervous enough about their precarious position—and that was before she'd begun to worry about the risks Kirk might take on her behalf. "Did you want to play again?"

"I suppose." Kirk shifted position and winced.

His obvious suffering from his cracked rib sent a spear of guilt stabbing through Stasi. She'd realized while he was gone to Sardis that she needed to apologize for the way she'd treated him the last six years. But it was difficult to find the words. She cleared her throat.

"I appreciate everything that you've done—not just rescuing me, but also—" She pulled up the courage to look up from the chessboard, and found his eyes on her face. Her breath caught.

"Also?" he prompted her, his deep voice so low she might have missed it if she hadn't seen the word fall from his lips.

He'd always had nice lips.

She chased the thought from her mind. "Also, what you did for my brother. I blamed you for taking him away, even though I knew deep down that you wouldn't do anything to hurt him. I was angry—mad at him for leaving, mad at you for helping him leave. And I didn't understand why he had to go, and why you wouldn't give me a straight answer to any of my questions."

"If I could have answered them, I would have." Sincerity glimmered in his eyes.

"I believe you. At the time, I couldn't imagine what could possibly be so bad that you wouldn't explain everything to me. But after witnessing the attack on the motorcade, and fleeing for our lives.…" Emotion caught in her throat. She shook her head. "It's bad, isn't it? Why Thad left—why the insurgents attacked us?"

"It's bad."

"Why would my father do something like this?"

"Stasi—" Kirk shuffled toward her, wincing as he did so "—your father didn't do this. He made some choices—I don't know a lot of the details, but as I understand it, he got himself backed into a corner. He thought he had no way out. By the time he told your brother what was happening, there *was* no way out. Thad left as a matter of principle. He couldn't undo what your father did, but he wouldn't be a part of it, either."

"So he left us to fend for ourselves?"

"No. He left to keep you safe. And he didn't leave you alone." Kirk's eyes met hers. In spite of the injury to his ribs, he'd been leaning closer to her across the game board as they'd spoken. "He left you in my care."

Stasi's face felt hot. The sun had peaked in the sky and shined down on them, but she sensed the warmth that flooded her had more to do with Kirk's words and his proximity than the glowing orb above them.

"What do you mean?"

"I haven't been stalking you, if that's what you're afraid of. But I've always watched out for you, even when you were little. And with Thad gone and Alexander training half the time with the military in who-knows-where, and your sister on all her mission trips, you needed someone in your corner. Remember when your folks didn't want you studying gemology in the States?"

"They changed their minds overnight. I never understood why."

"I didn't threaten them that time—just reminded them that they'd let your siblings choose their own area of study."

"*That* time? Did you ever threaten them?"

The touch of a smile played with the corner of Kirk's mouth, though the rest of his expression was grim. "After your father got your sister engaged to that awful Greek billionaire, there were murmurs around the palace, and a visit from another billionaire. He was a dozen years older than you are. I can't imagine what they were thinking."

Stasi's felt her eyes widen. "I knew about some of that. It gave me the worst feeling of dread in the pit of my stomach. They wanted me to come home. I purposely missed my flight back."

"It's a good thing you did. That gave me the chance to talk to them. I simply reminded them their children would rather disappear than follow an ill-advised plan." The smile faded from Kirk's mouth, replaced by a stern look. "I always respected your parents, but some of the things your father did…" He shook his head and sighed. "It's a big responsibility, running a country. It's not my place to judge."

Gratitude overwhelmed Stasi, and she leaned the last couple of inches toward Kirk, wrapping one arm gently around his shoulder, squeezing him in a hug. "Thank you," she whispered, a moment before realizing how close she'd come to him, and the odd stirring of affection she felt toward him.

She pulled back quickly, and Kirk, too, looked uncomfortable.

He cleared his throat. "Perhaps I should check the phone again. There might be a message."

While Kirk punched buttons on his phone, Stasi put the chess game away. As she held the rook in her hand and considered how quickly Kirk had sacrificed the game piece, she couldn't help but see the parallels to his behaviors. He'd put himself on the line for her brother, and also for her. She felt guilty enough knowing how he'd suffered for each of them. She'd never forgive herself if something worse happened to him on her account.

And yet, as the blank face of the chess piece stared back at her, Stasi considered the unknowns of the path ahead of them and shivered. She couldn't let Kirk sacrifice himself for her.

A sudden cry from Kirk had Stasi fearing his rib injury had worsened. But when she spun around to see the bright hope on his face, she nearly fell on top of him trying to read the screen on the phone he held toward her.

ISABELLE IN SARDIS MEETING W/ PARLIAMENT

If she hadn't just experienced the awkwardness of hugging Kirk, she might have tried to embrace him again. It didn't escape Stasi's notice that Kirk's father hadn't attempted to encode his message. He wasn't communicating classified information, then. Isabelle's meeting with Parliament must have been common knowledge. "She's meeting with Parliament. It must be okay, then. Can we go home?"

"It sounds like it. Let me call my father."

Kirk dialed the phone with trembling fingers. His father answered immediately, but his tone didn't sound nearly as excited as Kirk might have hoped.

"It's over already," his father moaned.

"What is? Is Isabelle okay?"

"I don't know. We've not been told much, but the meeting was brief, and when they showed the clip of her on the news going to the car, she looked as though she might faint. Rumors are swirling. The matter is far from settled."

"Do you think it's safe for Stasi to return? She'd love to see her sister."

Silence.

"Father?"

"Personally—" Albert Covington seemed to be weighing his words carefully "—I think Isabelle may have walked into a trap. If Stasi wants to see her sister, we may be able to make it happen, but don't let anyone know it's her. Come tonight. Don't let anyone see you. Hopefully the situation will improve before nightfall, but I fear…"

"What?" Kirk felt a sense of dread creep up on him. Perhaps he should have established a code with his father, as well. Already he regretted openly discussing the princess.

"You don't want to know my fears. Just be careful, whatever you do. Your mother and I love you."

"I love you, too." Kirk closed the call and wished he didn't have to meet Stasi's eyes. But she had to have picked up enough from his end of the conversation to know the situation hadn't been resolved.

"Is it safe?" Stasi asked, the moment Kirk looked up at her.

"Not really," he admitted, "but it's not safe here, either. We need to get off this island."

Stasi didn't balk at his words. "How soon are we leaving?"

"Tonight. As soon as it gets dark."

Stasi had never been much for killing time, but waiting for nightfall to enact Kirk's plan was nearly driving her crazy with worry.

"Are you sure you'll be strong enough? I can't have you passing out on me," she asked for the fifth time.

And for the fifth time, Kirk made no promises. "I won't be recovered for another month or more, and we don't have the luxury of waiting. Not when that helicopter could return at any time. If they find you here there will be no escape, and I am in no condition to defend you. I won't let you fall into their hands."

As he spoke, Kirk headed for his boat, grimacing as he raised his arms to pull himself aboard.

Stasi rushed to stop him before he hurt himself. "Here, let me help. What are you after?"

"In the cabin, under the seat cushions, starboard side, there should be a set of sheets."

"What do you want with them?"

"I'd like to bind my ribs before we leave. We don't know what's ahead of us, and I don't want the rib to become displaced—that could cause internal injuries."

Stasi placed a gentle hand on Kirk's arm. "Stay here. I'll find the sheets and help you. You can't bind your own ribs."

She clambered about and quickly located the sheets, tearing one into thick strips at his instruction. Fortunately, the shirt he wore was the button-down variety, so she was able to help him take it off without lifting his arms above his head. She gasped when she saw the extent of his bruises in full daylight.

"What did they do to you?"

"Not as much as they might have."

Stasi gathered up the first strip of cloth and tried to decide how best to go about the delicate matter of trying to wrap the bands of cloth around him without hurting him. She'd hoped it could be accomplished by simply walking round and wrapping him like a maypole, but he would have none of that.

"I'm going to inhale as much as possible to my lungs. Then, quickly wrap it around me as snugly as you can. When I exhale, it will be that much tighter."

Stasi did her best, but when Kirk inhaled, he shook his head. "It's got to hold my ribs in place. What if we have to run—or worse yet, fight? I can't be worried about my broken rib breaking free and lacerating my lungs."

Much as Stasi prayed their adventures that evening wouldn't go that far, she knew his concerns were valid. So she took a deep breath and held the end of the fabric clamped to his side farthest from the injury. Then she extended her arms around his back, passing the length of cloth into her other hand, essentially embracing him. Though he was a tall, well-muscled man with very broad shoulders, his torso tapered considerably around his waist, permitting her to reach her hands all the way around him without difficulty.

Unless she thought about the difficulty of having her arms wrapped around a handsome man in such a manner. It wasn't as much a difficulty as it was a distraction, but she turned all her attention toward making the binding as snug as possible.

"That's not too tight? I'm not pinching you?" She paused once she had it three times around, half expecting him to protest that she'd gone too far.

Instead, he smiled, and she watched as he inhaled slowly, testing his breath. "That's just right. Do another stretch a little higher, and then one more over them both to secure it. That should hold."

Stasi knotted the cloth in place and repeated the process, focusing on following Kirk's instructions, and not thinking about the tender way his eyes followed her as she worked. "Are you sure that's not too tight?" She knotted the last band of cloth firmly in place, and looked up to see Kirk's eyes dancing with merriment.

"Are you thinking about the time you put a Band-Aid on your finger too tight, and your finger turned blue from lack of circulation?"

Stasi felt her mouth drop open. She *had* been thinking about that very incident—though it hadn't crossed her mind in years.

"I believe, at the time," Kirk continued, "I told you if you didn't loosen it up, your finger might fall off."

"I couldn't let that happen," Stasi reminded him. "It was my ring finger."

A moment's awareness snapped between them, but Kirk blinked and the moment was gone. He gestured with one hand toward the bands she'd tied around him. "This is different."

"I wouldn't be so sure." She tried to match the teasing tone she'd heard in his voice. "You might turn blue and pass out, and then how will I ever be reunited with my family?"

"You'd make it just fine. I have faith in you."

Somewhere in the middle of his statement, the lighthearted tone disappeared, and his expression became one of earnest sincerity.

Stasi felt the need to correct his overestimation of her capability. "I'm not strong and brave like you are."

"You're tenacious—always have been."

"Hardly. Are you forgetting all the times you had to carry me around as a kid because I couldn't keep up with the others?"

"You're forgetting—" Kirk leaned a little closer "—the only reason I carried you so much was because you refused to be left behind. You'd scramble after all us bigger kids, and you wouldn't give up. You *are* strong and brave."

Stasi blinked and tried to think of a response, but her mind seemed stuck on how close Kirk stood to her, how the cuts and bruises on his face did nothing to detract from his handsomeness, and how she wanted so much to believe his words were true.

*Me—strong and brave?* She hadn't even been able to get out of her own bedroom without help. A few out-of-place necklaces had been enough to frighten her. "Thank you," she whispered, finally finding her feet and managing to step away from Kirk. "I don't think you're right, but I appreciate your kind words."

Kirk felt frustrated by his injury. He hated that Stasi had to do all the grunt work of sailing his boat back toward Sardis, but she insisted he sit still and not move, and he knew he was in no condition to protest. If he was going to do a decent job of protecting her, he couldn't risk injuring himself over something as inconsequential as the angle of the jib sail. So she clambered around the boat keeping everything pointed in more or less the right direction, and he told himself it would have to be good enough.

Good enough to get them into port at Sardis, and that was all he needed.

She leaped about in the darkness, her black slacks and button-down shirt camouflaging her against the dark night sky. Even her low-heeled boots were black, and the dark kerchief she'd tied around her blond hair gave her a sort of monochrome pirate look as she set the sails.

Princess Anastasia was an exceptional woman, and Kirk fought against the pinch near his heart—the one that didn't come from his ribs. Watching her gave him a melancholy, bittersweet feeling. Like the jewels she'd worn the night of the ambush, Stasi was a treasure—sparkling, beautiful…and not his. Kirk reminded himself that it was an honor to spend time in her presence. That was enough.

Not only did the gutsy girl bring them into port at the dock in Sardis, but Stasi even managed to tie the boat securely, and help him keep his feet as he struggled to disembark without dislocating his cracked rib.

"Steady?" She buttressed his left side firmly.

"I am now. Thank you." He'd already warned her about the possibility of encountering soldiers—he didn't want a repeat of what had happened two nights before. So he took care to be certain there was no one around. "I don't see anyone. Let's hurry."

He felt stiff as he focused on keeping his torso as still as possible, while at the same time, practically running down the dock. He'd arranged for his father to meet them with a car, and was pleased to see yellow running lights illumine, fade, and then illumine again—his father's signal that the coast was clear.

A small hand took his, and Staci tugged him in the direction of the car. She knew the signal, but her sudden touch still surprised him, not only with the trust it communicated, but by the thrill he felt holding her hand.

Stasi practically dived into the backseat, and Kirk managed to clamber in after her without upsetting his injury. Stasi had done a wonderful job binding his ribs.

As he gingerly eased back to grab the door and pull it shut, Stasi reached across him and closed it for him. She gave him an understanding smile as she settled back into her seat.

His heart gave a funny leap, which he realized had nothing to do with the tight bands that compressed his chest and everything to do with the woman who'd tied them. He needed to keep a clear head.

"Your mother has something to show you." Albert Covington spoke from the front seat as he pointed the car up the familiar roads toward the palace.

"Is it good or bad?" Kirk couldn't tell from his father's tone.

"We're not sure. Hopefully Her Highness will be able to answer that question."

Kirk wasn't sure what his father meant being so mysterious, but he figured he wouldn't have long to wait. Already the car approached the side gates of the palace grounds, which his father opened via remote control.

"Are you sure we'll be safe this close to the palace?" Kirk clarified.

His father pointed the car through the open gates without flinching. "As you said yourself, most Lydians are loyal to the crown. The insurgents can't go after all of them. If we keep our heads down, there's no safer place than right here inside the palace walls."

Between the Covingtons' small garage and their cottage, a row of pine trees shielded the walkway from view. Between that and the midnight darkness, Kirk and Stasi made it into his parents' kitchen without any difficulty.

"Kirk!" Theresa Covington jumped up from the kitchen table and reached for him.

Raising his hands to ward her off, Kirk managed to avoid an embrace that would only bring pain to his injured ribs.

His mother turned her attention instead to Stasi, wrapping the petite princess in her motherly embrace while shaking her head disapprovingly at Kirk. "You look awful. What have they done to you?"

Though his shirt covered the worst of his injuries, Kirk believed his mother's assessment of his appearance. "It's a long story. I'm more interested in hearing if there's any news. Where's Isabelle?"

"As far as anyone knows she's still in town, but there's been no news since her brief appearance at Parliament this morning." His mother gave Stasi an apologetic look, obviously finding the whole situation regrettable. "Word is, she was taken to the American ambassador's residence."

"Ambassador Valli?" Stasi looked indignant. "Isabelle can't stand Valli. He arranged her engagement to that awful Greek billionaire, and then maligned her when she broke it off. What is she doing staying at his residence?"

Albert and Theresa Covington exchanged worried looks. Theresa shook her head. "We don't know. Your sister may be in an awful fix."

"And we still don't know who's behind the attacks?" Kirk clarified.

"Dozens of rumors and theories, but nothing that's been substantiated." Albert turned to his wife. "Should we show them?"

"Yes!" Theresa practically leaped through the doorway to the dining room to the locked drawer of the china cabinet. She pulled a key from her pocket, opened the drawer and gingerly removed a paper-bound package, presenting it to Stasi with a solemn expression.

"This arrived earlier today, express from Milan. See the date?"

Kirk squinted over Stasi's shoulder at the code that revealed the date and time the package was mailed. "The evening of the attacks?"

His mother nodded. "And see who it's addressed to?"

"Genevieve Watkins?" Stasi read aloud, the name obviously unfamiliar to her.

His mother gave them a knowing look. "Watkins was Queen Elaine's maiden name."

"And Genevieve?" Kirk asked.

"Philip wanted to name their fourth child Genevieve. Elaine wanted to name her Anastasia, but she was going to go along with what Philip wanted. Then, when she almost died giving birth, Philip decided to follow his wife's wishes and call her Anastasia after all."

Kirk wasn't completely certain he followed his mother's explanation, though it sent a creeping fear up the back of his neck. "I don't understand. Who sent the package?"

"Who could have sent it? I believe it came from the queen."

# SIX

"My mother?" Stasi tried to ignore the sudden hammering of her heart. "You think she may have survived the attack?"

Theresa pointed to the name on the package. "What else could this mean?"

Stasi shook her head. "You think *I'm* Genevieve Watkins?" She'd heard the woman's explanation, but it was all too far-fetched for her to believe—especially after all the disappointments she'd suffered of late.

But Kirk's mother nodded solemnly. "Elaine knows I handle the royal mail, so she no doubt knew I would be the one to sign for the package. Albert and I may be the only people besides the king and queen themselves who were aware Philip had intended to name you Genevieve."

"Why don't you open it?" Kirk suggested.

Nodding, Stasi carefully undid the tape, trying her best not to tear anything. She was almost afraid to see what was inside. After several layers of thick brown paper, she came to several more layers of tissue paper. Once she peeled them back, she nearly screamed.

"What is it?" Kirk asked.

It took Stasi a moment to answer. Could it be? It didn't seem possible. Yet the diamonds and teardrop amethysts twinkled up at her with the utmost sincerity. She held the package open for everyone to see. "The crown jewels. My mother was planning to wear them to the state dinner."

The sky lurched above her and her vision blurred.

"Sit down." Kirk's voice cut through the rushing sound in her ears, and he pulled out a kitchen chair behind her. "Breathe. Slowly." He took the package from her and placed it open on the table.

Stasi did as she was told, realizing only as the world began to right itself that she'd very nearly fainted. "No. No. No." It took a moment longer before she recognized the stammering voice as her own. Her eyes focused on ceiling above them. She couldn't look at the crown jewels. Not yet.

"Your mother *was* wearing them," Theresa assured her. "I helped her clasp the necklace myself."

"No. It can't be." Stasi managed to look at the jewels again. "They don't show any sign of trauma. There's no damage." She picked up the necklace her mother had supposedly been wearing at the time of the attack two days before and turned over the central jewel to reveal the hidden locket on the back plate, which she snapped open with her thumbnail, revealing the key that always hung there, undisturbed in its hiding place. If anyone had tried to create a replica of the royal jewels from a photograph, they wouldn't have known about the hidden locket or the secret key concealed inside. Yet it didn't seem possible that the necklace could have survived. "There's not even a scratch on them."

Kirk looked at her patiently. "Your mother had to have sent them."

Stasi struggled to wrap her head around the idea. Her mother. Alive. In Milan? "But you saw the blasts. You saw them hit the motorcade. It's possible someone may have survived, but for their jewelry to look like it was just pulled from its case?" She shook her head. "Don't forget—I studied gemology. I took an entire course on the indicators of wear and use. These are in perfect condition."

"Well then." Theresa's voice sounded far too cheerful. "Your mother must be in perfect condition, too."

"In Milan?" Granted, her mother loved the town, and Stasi visited there often. "Why there, when all of us are struggling to sort out this mess over here? What's she doing in Milan?"

"Apparently trying to contact you." Albert picked up the brown wrapper the jewelry had arrived in, and smoothed out the label that bore the palace address. "And going to great lengths not to be found out."

"There's got to be a note." Stasi sifted through the tissue paper. "She's got to have sent some form of instruction." Her search became more frantic as she turned over every bit of paper in the package and found nothing.

Theresa let out a labored sigh over her shoulder. "She can't have risked it. Don't you see? She couldn't be certain these would reach you. If a message fell into the wrong hands…"

"You're right," Albert agreed with his wife. "There won't be a message. The *jewels* are the message."

"Oh!" Theresa gasped. "Stasi, you studied jewels in college. Your mother must have known you'd understand."

Stasi blinked down at the teardrop gems. "Teardrops." She touched the shapes reverently, "For tears. For mourning. I asked my mother once why the crown jewels of our nation are in the shape of teardrops."

"Why?" Theresa urged.

Exhaling a slow breath, Stasi struggled to keep her voice steady. "On Easter morning, Mary Magdalene wept at the tomb of Jesus. Jesus appeared to her himself, alive, and her tears of mourning were turned to tears of joy. That is why the crown jewels of Lydia bear the teardrop form. Our people live in the joy of the risen Lord."

Kirk cleared his throat. "Your mother is telling you she's alive, then? And not to weep or mourn or lose hope?"

Stasi shook her head. "But why would she send them to me? How did she know I survived the attack? How could she risk letting the most valuable jewels in the kingdom fall into the wrong hands?"

"Perhaps she didn't *know* you'd survived the attack," Albert suggested. "Perhaps she simply *hoped* you had."

"She may have had no other choice." Kirk rose to standing and began to pace. "She must have felt the risk of mailing them was less dangerous than keeping them with her."

"But why?" Stasi couldn't sort it out.

"What else do the crown jewels signify?" Theresa asked.

"The monarchy." Stasi pointed out the most obvious thing. "When my father was crowned king and my mother queen, she was crowned with this tiara." Stasi lifted it from the nest of tissue paper and stiff cardboard that had protected it in transit.

"You don't think?" Kirk looked back and forth between his parents.

It took Stasi a moment to guess what he was thinking. "You don't think, by sending these, she's telling us she's abdicating?"

"I pray not." Kirk spun around and found his mother's laptop at the workstation in the corner of the kitchen. He quickly searched for news on the situation in Lydia, while explaining to Stasi, "Your mother doesn't have ruling power anyway. Hers is a token title because she married your father. For her to abdicate means little."

He found the latest headlines on the Lydian events and clicked on one that covered Isabelle's meeting with Parliament that morning. He scanned the first few paragraphs and let out a frustrated breath.

"What?" Stasi rested her gentle hands on his shoulders as she peered past him at the screen. "Is it about the crown?"

"Yes. Parliament cannot meet or conduct official business without the authority of the crown. With your father gone, they're pressing to crown someone else."

"Someone *else?* But there are rules of succession. It has to be a direct descendent of Lydia—the founder of the church of Lydia from chapter sixteen of the Book of Acts in the Bible. It has to be one of *us.* Thad was next in line after my father. With him gone, my brother Alexander would be next, and Isabelle after him, and lastly me. Why didn't Parliament just crown Isabelle when she was there earlier today?"

"That's just it." Kirk highlighted a relevant paragraph for Stasi to read. "Your great-grandfather, Alexander the Third, had an older half-brother, Basil. Basil's mother died when he was born, but their father was the prince and heir to the throne, so both sons are legitimate descendants of Lydia."

"Basil *abdicated.*" Stasi's long curls brushed the side of Kirk's face as she shook her head adamantly. "He ran off to America and married a Greek actress, and died a few years later. Once a ruler abdicates, their claim to the throne is dissolved, and the line of the new ruler is followed. There's no jumping back and forth."

Kirk highlighted the next paragraph and waited for Stasi to catch up.

"No," she protested. "They're calling Basil's abdication into question? His descendants claim theirs is the rightful line?" Her fingers gripped Kirk's shoulder tightly.

"Basil had a daughter who had three sons." Kirk spun his chair around to face her. "If their claim is correct, Basil's grandsons would be next in line to the throne."

Stasi shook her head. "With my father gone…"

"But he's not gone." Albert dangled a teardrop amethyst earring in front of both of them. "Don't you remember the teardrops? Mary Magdalene wept because she thought Jesus was dead. But he wasn't dead. That's the message. *They're not dead.*"

Stasi looked from the twinkling gem to Kirk and back to the laptop screen. "What is Parliament going to do?"

Kirk clicked back to the page of headlines. Already a new headline screamed at them from the top of the list.

Lydian Coronation Scheduled

With a sinking heart he opened the article and read aloud, "'In the absence of King Philip, Parliament has scheduled the coronation of the new Lydian King, Stephanos Valli, for ten o'clock tomorrow morning, Lydian time.'" Kirk glanced at the clock. "That's in ten hours."

"Stephanos Valli?" Stasi protested. "The American ambassador? Why him?"

Kirk swallowed. "He's Basil's grandson."

Stasi met his eyes. "What? Why has he been serving as ambassador all this time if he thought he was in line with the throne? Why come out with all this now? He's got to be in league with the insurgents."

"I don't doubt that he is. If his claim was legitimate, he should have brought it up with your whole family here. If he's waited until your family was out of the picture to come forward, I can't help but think his claim lacks legitimacy. We can't let the coronation move forward."

"But what can you do?" Theresa wailed from behind them. "You can't change the mind of Parliament. Your sister already tried. She met with Parliament, and they're still planning to crown Valli."

"But he's got to be behind this mess." Albert still had the earring, and waved it about for emphasis. "He's been plotting things for years, with those engagements, and knowing all this time that he was descended from the reigning line. He knew Philip was the only one standing between him and the crown. Don't think he's not the one who tried to knock him off."

Stasi plucked the earring from Albert's waving hand. "There's only one person who can challenge Valli's right to rule. My father." She clutched the little earring and stared at it. "If he's not dead, we've got to get him and bring him back."

"But where are you going to find him?" Theresa asked.

"Milan." Stasi pointed to the postmark on the brown paper packaging.

"But it's a city of over a million people," Albert objected. "And you don't even have a return address. All you've got is a postmark."

Stasi gave them all a desperate look, and for a moment, Kirk was afraid she might cry.

He stood and cupped her shoulders in his hands. "You know the city. You know their haunts. Can you find them?"

She met his eyes and the trust in their dazzling blue depths took his breath away. "I think I can."

"But how are you going to get there?" Theresa asked. "It's over a thousand kilometers across the Adriatic Sea, and then over a hundred more kilometers by land. Even if you could sail there, you'd never make it before the coronation."

A familiar thrumming sound stole Kirk's attention, and he crossed the room to the back door, opening it and looking outside.

"What is it?" Stasi poked her head out next to his arm.

"It's a helicopter. It must be beyond those trees—somewhere in the vicinity of Idyllia Park, I'd guess."

"Wait!" Stasi grabbed his arm. "A *helicopter*."

Distracted as he was by the closeness of the princess and the emotions she stirred up every time she touched him, Kirk could only ask, "What about it?"

"A helicopter would get us to Milan quickly."

"If it had the fuel capacity. Milan is a long way for a helicopter to fly. Even straight as the crow flies it's a thousand kilometers."

"The royal helicopters can make it. Mother and I regularly made the trip without stopping to refuel. Father special ordered the helicopters with that very trip in mind."

"But, Your Highness—" Kirk didn't want to disappoint the princess, especially when she looked so hopeful "—we don't have a helicopter."

Stasi barely blinked. "Yes, we do. They belong to my family—purchased with our own private money, and not the peoples' taxes."

Though there were plenty more objections he could make, Kirk only sighed. He already knew how tenacious—and stubborn—the princess could be. And she had that determined look in her eye.

She pulled him back into the room and closed the door against the fading sounds of the helicopter. "You can fly one, can't you Kirk?"

"I've only ever flown as copilot," he reminded her.

"Yes, with old Elias." Stasi rolled her eyes. "Propped up in the pilot's seat. We both know you were the one keeping the helicopter in the sky."

"But there's the problem of access," Kirk reminded her. "The helipad is on the roof of the royal guard's headquarters—possibly the most secure point in the whole city. It's not as though we can just walk up and take one."

"*You* can. You're a member of the royal guard. Your thumbprint will get us in."

"My thumbprint will tell everyone that *I'm* the one who's just walked through the door—and that's assuming they haven't already removed me from the system, or worse yet, flagged me to set off an internal alarm the next time I check in. I got a cracked rib the last time a royal guard recognized me. It could be worse if they recognize me again."

Stasi took hold of his arm again, and this time fairly hugged it. "I don't think they'll have thought of all that yet. And we've got to try. My mother sent us the jewels for a reason. We can't let Stephanos Valli be crowned. If he's done all these terrible things just to get the crown, imagine what he'll do once he has it."

More than the tug on his arm, Kirk felt Stasi's tug on his heart. She'd made several excellent points. And ultimately, it wasn't up to him to make the call. "Is that an order, Your Highness?"

She met his eyes for a long moment. "No, it's not an order. It's a request from a friend."

He studied her face. She had every right as a member of the royal family to tell him, a member of the royal guard, what to do. But she hadn't used that privilege. Somehow, her decision closed the gap between them a tiny bit more.

"All right," he said softly, "but we'll have to move quickly." He left the *or else* of his statement unspoken. They all knew what was hanging in the balance, and what awful risks they'd be taking to get to Milan.

Stasi tried to think of everything they might need. While Kirk recharged his phone battery, Theresa sneaked back into the palace to fetch Stasi's passport and her international driving permit. If they were going to travel anywhere after they reached Milan, they'd need both of them.

Albert tried to help Kirk get his holster on over his shoulder, but Kirk winced and shook his head. "I can't reach my gun without twisting around anyway, and that's bound to be a problem. Besides, I might get into trouble for wearing a gun."

Kirk's father looked concerned, and Stasi got the impression the older man was reluctant to let them go on with their plan.

"You've got to keep her highness safe *from every threat*." Father and son looked at each other earnestly, and Stasi wondered at the seriousness of what passed between them. Was Albert telling Kirk something beyond the obvious?

Kirk's lips were set in the firm line. "I've already promised you. I will."

His father nodded solemnly. "What about money? If either of you use a credit card, those in high places may be able to track you down. I wouldn't underestimate who you're up against."

"That's a valid concern," Kirk agreed.

"I should be able to get cash for us." Stasi had already considered the issue. "I have friends of some means in Milan."

When Theresa returned from the palace, she insisted on packing them a small cooler with food and bottled water, but wouldn't hand it over when Kirk reached for it. "Let's pray first."

Stasi bowed her head, but before she got her fingers folded, Albert took one of her hands, and Stasi saw they were making a circle, holding hands to pray. She looked tentatively at the hand Kirk offered her—a strong, capable hand—and was glad to take it.

By the time they finished praying, Stasi had tears running down her cheeks. "I'm so grateful for your family." She wiped at her eyes. "You've all done so much for me."

"Your family has done that and more for us," Theresa countered.

"We put your son through an awful trial." Stasi shook her head regretfully.

"That was a difficult time," Theresa acknowledged. "But God held us through that, and He'll hold us through this, too. Have faith."

With that, there was nothing more to do but take their lunch and the small overnight bag each of them had packed, and head across the courtyard toward the guard station.

Stasi had always loved the many gracious shade trees that filled the back garden of the palace grounds. As a child, she'd run after Kirk countless times, and been carried by him more times than that. Now she darted from tree to tree in his shadow, the game so much more frightening than any they'd played as children, and the stakes so much higher.

And back then, they'd never ventured as close to the royal guard's headquarters as they were going tonight. They ducked behind the last large tree before the open driveway that led to the chain-link fence surrounding the square stone building.

Stasi leaned close to Kirk, trying to disappear as much as possible into his shadow. He'd shaved before they'd left his parent's house, and the scent of his aftershave tickled her nose.

Kirk didn't seem to be paying any attention to her. He kept his back straight as he peeked past the crook of a branch, scoping out their target.

He'd already briefed her on the guard rotation, and worn his midnight-blue night uniform in case there might be any benefit to blending in. But Stasi knew Kirk was bigger than most of the guards. She'd always been able to recognize him from the back, even in the years when she hadn't wanted to. There was no doubt in her mind that if anyone spotted them, they'd be instantly recognized, guard uniform or not. It might buy them a few seconds and the benefit of the doubt on a fuzzy surveillance video, but that was about it.

And there would be no explaining away *her* presence.

His fingers found hers and wrapped securely around them. "Ready?"

She looked up to his mouth mere inches from her eyes.

When had he moved so close to her? Or had she moved close to him? She took a deep breath and tried not to think about the lips so near to hers, or Kirk's intriguing scent. "Ready."

He gave her hand a squeeze, dropped it and, as planned, walked toward the chain-link fence with a casual stride.

Kirk pressed his thumb against the security panel.

Green.

They were in.

But how far would they get before they were recognized? There was another checkpoint at the building, and then a third at the very top of the stairs, before they could access the helipad on the roof. And any number of guards stood between them.

She followed Kirk to the back door of the security building and prayed while he pressed his thumb to the next panel.

It seemed to take forever to register.

Had they set off an alarm? Would they be trapped between the gate and the building?

Green.

Finally, Stasi let out the breath she was holding and followed Kirk inside. So far, so good. She hadn't seen anyone.

Kirk moved down a side hall, which he'd explained would be the least-traveled route to the back stairs. But that left them with another length of hallway to travel before they'd reach the stairs to the roof.

Her heart beat quickly, not so much from the exertion of climbing the stairs but, she was sure, from the mounting fear she felt walking through enemy territory. They stepped around the corner at the top of the stairs and were greeted by a flash of red light.

A red orb several centimeters in diameter blinked silently from a box on the wall, its glaring light filling the hallway with harsh, strobing color.

Kirk made an angry noise in his throat, grabbed her hand and started down the hall at a run.

Six paces later a guard stepped into the hallway in front of them, his arm outstretched toward them. "Kirk Covington!" he ordered. "Stop where you are."

# SEVEN

Stasi nearly ran into Kirk as he skidded to a stop.

"Galen." Kirk addressed the guard.

The man blinked rapidly. "Two figures were spotted on the security camera. I've been sent to investigate." He swallowed and leaned closer. "What would I report if you were to get past me?"

Kirk took a step closer to the man. "Tell them you were overpowered."

"Blacken my eye."

When Kirk hesitated, Galen's voice grew more desperate. "Hurry, before they dispatch more guards. I can't let them think you got away without a fight. I'd be in a far greater world of hurt then."

Kirk nodded solemnly, braced his left arm against his right side as though to hold his ribs in place, drew back, and knocked Galen in the eye.

Galen stumbled back. "You could have hit me harder than that."

But Kirk had Stasi's hand again and pulled her down the hall. She suspected he couldn't have punched the man any harder, not without hurting himself. They ran up the last flight of stairs and, to her relief, his thumbprint got them through to the roof.

The copter waited, hulking like a massive raptor in the darkness.

Kirk threw their things on board before offering Stasi his hand to climb in. Though she might have thought she ought to be the one helping him in his injured condition, there was no time to protest. She climbed inside and waited, tense, while Kirk settled into the pilot's seat and started flipping switches.

"Give it a minute to power up," he said, as the panel of lights came on and the rotors began to swish above them.

Kirk pulled down the headsets that dangled from harness clips above them, and helped Stasi adjust hers over her ears so they could speak to one another comfortably over the ambient roar.

She buckled herself into the copilot's seat and watched as Kirk quickly ran checks of the various gauges.

"We've got a full tank." He sounded relieved. "We'll need every drop."

Red glare reflected off the bright lights of the instruments, and Stasi glanced behind them in time to see a red alarm light flashing above the door to the roof.

"They're on to us," she warned Kirk.

"I need ten more seconds." His eyes stayed focused on the climbing numbers in front of him as the rotors began to turn faster and faster above their heads.

"You may not have ten seconds." She watched as the door opened behind them. "Kirk!"

"Five, four, three…"

Men seemed to pour through the door faster than Kirk could count. But before one could reach them, he grabbed the controls and they lifted off.

Stasi looked back in time to see a guard pull out his gun. But just as quickly, another guard grabbed the man's arm, and then they were too high in the sky for Stasi to see anything.

"Oh, thank God," Stasi prayed.

"Keep praying." Kirk didn't look away from what he was doing at the controls, but flipped a switch and winced at the digital number that shone back at him. "We're going to need all the fuel in our tank to get to Milan. If we have to engage in any evasive maneuvers, we won't be able to make it there."

Kirk tried to convince Stasi to rest. It would take them over three hours to reach Milan, and he knew she hadn't slept since the sound of a helicopter had awakened them in the middle of the night the night before.

"You need your sleep. We still have a long journey ahead of us."

"I don't think I've ever been through so much excitement. I still keep expecting another aircraft to come after us at any moment." She leaned back into her seat, and when her eyes closed dutifully, Kirk thought she'd taken his advice to heart.

But a moment later, her blue eyes popped open again. "Why do you suppose that is?"

"What is?"

"That they didn't come after us? Don't you think we got away too easily?"

"Galen tried to stop us."

"No, he didn't. He let us through on purpose."

"He's a good kid. I changed a flat tire for him once."

Stasi rubbed her temples. "I still don't like it. Something's rotten in the royal guard."

"What do you mean?"

"If you hadn't let me out of my room, I wouldn't have been anywhere near the motorcade when it was ambushed."

"You don't think someone from the royal guard was behind that prank, do you?"

"It wasn't a prank. I don't know who was behind it, but the timing worries me. Did whoever barricade my door know about the ambush? If so, why would they want to keep me from it?"

Her questions hit him like a blow to the ribs, and he caught his breath. "If someone wanted the royal family dead, why would they keep *you* alive?"

"They must have had plans for me—something worse than death." She pulled in a slow breath. "Anyway, it's not the first time someone's trespassed in my room."

"That's right—you mentioned reporting the previous incidents, but I never saw a report about them. Was anything taken?"

"Not that I could ever prove. But things were out of place."

"What things?"

"A few clothes. Mostly my jewelry."

"My mother—"

"I talked to your mother first. Yes, she often puts my clothes away, but she and I have a system. This wasn't her. Besides, your mother never goes anywhere near my jewelry."

Kirk puzzled over the curious incidents. "How long were you gone from your room when it happened? Hours? Days?"

"A day or two at most. Once it couldn't have been more than a few hours."

"Do you think someone might have stolen your jewelry and replaced it with fakes?"

"I thought of that, but I examined the jewels myself. They were the originals."

For a few moments, Kirk studied the helicopter instruments, his mind pondering over the strange incidents. "Were they looking for something?"

"I can't think what it might have been."

"Why would they return? Surely they'd have figured out soon enough that they couldn't find it."

Stasi looked thoughtful. "It is an exceptionally large jewelry armoire. There are two dozen drawers, and most of those have lift-out trays with compartments underneath. It could take a person hours to go through the whole thing. And then, if they thought they'd missed something, or if they didn't have long to search, I could see them coming back. I just wish I knew what they were looking for."

Kirk's heart beat hard. Stasi was right—something was rotten, and he wished he could scent out what it was. "What about the crown jewels your mother sent you? Are you quite sure they're the originals?"

"I've been wondering about that, and how there wasn't a mark on them. From what I can tell looking at them, they're identical, right down to the hidden locket on the necklace and the key inside it. But I can't be sure unless I examine them with the proper instruments." She bit her bottom lip and looked thoughtful for a moment. "I have an idea. Before we look for my parents, we should stop by my favorite jewelry shop and have a look at the contents of that package. If they're not the real thing, we'll know something's up."

"But the stores won't be open yet when we first get to town, and I thought you were in a hurry to find your folks."

"I'm not in any hurry to walk into a trap. Too many strange things have happened, and too much is at stake. Besides, shop hours or not, my friend Giovanni will let us in."

"All right," Kirk agreed. Part of the reason he'd decided to go along with Stasi's plan to head for Milan was because he still felt she'd be safest far from Sardis. The last thing he wanted to do was walk into a trap. If visiting the jewelry shop would help them avoid that, he was all for it.

With the matter settled, Stasi sat back and slept as promised.

Kirk looked across at her, sleeping in her seat, her delicate cheekbones cast in a glow from the instruments, her blond hair all tied up and hidden away under the black kerchief she'd worn from the island.

*Anastasia.* She was beautiful. Of course she was. She was
a princess, and, he realized with a twinge of guilt, he had no
right to look at her while she slept.

He turned his attention to the unchanging night sky, and
pinched his lips into a firm line, as though he could as easily
squash all that he felt for her. He forced himself to recall his
father's words, *Keep her safe from every threat.* There was
no question what his father had meant. Though Albert Covington was no doubt aware of the dangers they faced from
their enemies, he'd always been acutely concerned about the
affection Kirk and Stasi felt for each other.

When Kirk was very young, his parents had often reminded him that the royal siblings were to be treated with
care and respect. Those cautions had only increased as he'd
grown older. It wasn't until he was twelve years old, carrying
a gangly legged seven-year-old Stasi on his shoulders during
a chase across the palace grounds, that he'd tripped and they'd
gone down in a tumble, laughing.

His father had come running and dragged him off by the
ear all the way to their cottage, and given him the lecture
of his life. Stasi's station was leagues above his own. He
couldn't display the slightest hint of impropriety. Whatever
friendliness they felt between them needed to be stomped
out.

Young as he was, Kirk hadn't understood then, but he'd
tried to erase their friendship as though it had never been.
For his father and mother's sake, he'd tried to treat Stasi no
differently than he treated Queen Elaine, though the little
princess had subjected him to no end of teasing because of
his stiff formality. She didn't understand the reason for the
change in his behavior, and Kirk hadn't been able to explain
it to her. It had taken him years understand it, though in some
ways, he wrestled with it still.

By the time Stasi was seventeen, Kirk had realized what

it was. There *was* something between them, an undercurrent of attraction that went beyond friendship. Once Thad disappeared, Kirk found it easier to ignore, since Stasi turned a cold shoulder on him. But now that she was back in his life, there it was—a longing that drew him no matter how hard he fought it. He'd won many a difficult battles in his time, but this one he had yet to conquer.

Still, he was determined. He would treat Stasi no differently than he treated the queen. He might not ever change the way he felt about the princess, but he would make certain he never acted on those feelings.

Kirk gripped the helicopter controls firmly. Stasi was royalty. He wasn't good enough for her. He would keep her safe from every threat, including the feelings he had for her.

They reached Milan shortly after dawn, and Kirk reluctantly nudged her arm to awaken her. "Where would you like me to put us down?"

"There's a lay-by near the hotel where my parents always stay, with a bus and taxi stop. It's only a couple of blocks from there to the jewelry shop."

"Are you quite certain we can pass from there undetected?"

"It's Milan, not Lydia. No one is looking for me here. And I still have my hair tied up." She pulled an oversize pair of sunglasses from her purse. "There. Satisfied?"

"It will have to do—but let's not be out in the open any longer than we have to."

He surveyed the neighborhood as they landed, but nothing looked out of place, and no one seemed to bat an eye as they disembarked from their helicopter and stretched their legs. A leathery old man looked up from where he swept the sidewalk in front of the bus stop and nodded in greeting.

Kirk smiled and nodded back.

Stasi had his hand, and fairly pulled him off down the street, which had barely begun to crawl to life at the early hour.

A few blocks later, at a handsome storefront under the sign Giovanni's, Stasi walked right past the metal security gates that protected the darkened windows, around to the back and buzzed a box on the wall.

A man's voice answered in Italian, and Kirk couldn't help smiling as exotic-sounding words slipped from the princess's sweet little mouth. Then she turned a triumphant smile up at him, a buzzer sounded, and they stepped inside.

A robust figure almost as leathery as the man they'd seen at the bus stop switched on a light and hurried forward to meet them.

"Ah, Anastasia!" He bowed and kissed Stasi's hand, running off in Italian at length, obviously relieved to see the princess alive.

Stasi's Italian didn't falter, and a moment later she pulled the package from her bag, and Giovanni's eyes went wide. He escorted the two of them out to the front room where expansive cases held a pirate's trove of treasures.

Giovanni snapped on a monocle that made his round eye look even rounder, and blinked intently at the gems. Then he chattered rapidly in Italian, leaving Kirk feeling woefully behind.

Stasi must have sensed it, because the next time Giovanni stopped for a breath, she inquired if they might not speak in English.

"Ah, *sì,* yes, Your Highness." He nodded. "These are your mother's stones—the crown jewels. I know them well. She brought them to me some years ago for cleaning. Very memorable. You know about the locket on the back of the central jewel." Giovanni opened the latch on the back plate of the large gem, revealing the tiny key inside.

"Yes." Stasi reached for the necklace and clasped the latch

securely shut again. "There is no doubt? It couldn't be a replica?"

"No, no doubt." Giovanni held out the stones on their bed of tissue paper wrapping. He pointed to the large teardrop shapes. "The color, the clarity—such a well-matched set, and the undertones of indigo give depth to the amethysts."

"I thought so, but I needed to be sure."

"Not even I could make its equal. They are a priceless treasure."

Stasi smiled, and Kirk felt as though the warmth of her smile lit up the room.

Giovanni pointed to a case of jewelry nearby. It didn't appear to be as full as the others. "And your collection is selling well. I will need more pieces if I am to keep up with demand."

Stasi blushed. "I haven't had time to work on new designs."

"Ah, you are a busy woman. So talented."

The princess shrugged the compliment away. "I have a favor to ask of you, Giovanni." She pulled another parcel from her bag, unwrapping the sapphire set she'd been wearing on the night of the attack. "I'd like to consign these."

Giovanni's eyes went wider, and protests spilled from his lips in a startled mixture of Italian and English.

Stasi shook her head firmly. "I've made up my mind."

"If it is funds you need," Giovanni offered, "I could pay you what you have earned for your work." He gestured toward the case that held her collection.

"You know our agreement." Stasi's blush deepened, and she shook her head, switching to Italian again.

Kirk couldn't help wondering what had made her blush so, or why she didn't want him to know the details of her arrangement with the jeweler. From what he could tell of the jewels in her collection, they were artfully designed and apparently quite popular. Like the princess herself, the jewelry looked delicate. He also knew precious stones were among the most indestructible substances in the world, having endured the tremendous pressure that created them.

They were also dreadfully expensive.

Kirk glanced back at Stasi. Like the gems she loved, she was way out of his league. He couldn't afford any of the nicer pieces in the case in front of him—and she, of course, deserved only the best.

It was the kind of reminder he sorely needed. However strong his feelings might be for her, they belonged in two different worlds, and her world came with a much higher price tag.

But at least it seemed Stasi had convinced her friend to take the sapphire jewelry set she'd brought.

"Fine. I will hold them for you." Giovanni opened up a safe under the back counter and pulled out an alarmingly large stack of bills. "I will give you cash against their value, but I will not try to sell them unless, heaven forbid…" He paused, folded his hands, and murmured a prayer, his eyes pointed heavenward.

Kirk watched Giovanni count out a large stack of banknotes to Stasi—in euros, the same currency used in Lydia, so Kirk had an idea of how much it was worth, even though he respectfully turned his head away.

Stasi hugged her old friend goodbye, and after he wished them well, she followed Kirk out the back door. The princess shoved at least half the stack of money at him.

"Have you got a discreet place to carry this?"

Kirk thought about confessing that the money was far more than he made in a year, and he couldn't replace it if he lost it, but like so many other details that might have seemed important any other day, the value of the money now felt utterly trivial. It was a means to an end. If the money helped them get King Philip back on his throne and the princess back in her palace, he would carry as much as she asked him to.

Besides, one other question had stuck in his head, and as they turned back up the road to the hotel Stasi had said her parents favored, Kirk decided to go ahead and ask it.

"Your jewelry collection—why have I never heard of it?"

When Stasi blushed, Kirk almost regretted asking.

But she was so adorable when she blushed.

"It's not exactly a matter of pride." Her downcast eyes may have been in an effort to keep her feet, but he suspected there was more to it than that. "The jewelry sells well enough without my name attached to it. I don't wish to draw attention to it."

"What does the money go to?"

"How do you—"

"You said Giovanni had an agreement with you about where the money from your jewelry sales is supposed to go."

A break in traffic allowed them to cross the street, and Stasi hurried on ahead of him.

Kirk had to rush to keep up. He thought she might be going to avoid his question, but after another adorable blush, she admitted, "You know my sister sponsors a mission, building deep-water wells in Africa. I wanted to accompany her, but the royal doctors insist I'm not strong enough to travel there."

Kirk nodded, understanding. Stasi had been born before her lungs had fully developed. They'd given her problems ever since. And Princess Isabelle traveled to some of the most disease-prone parts of Africa. Though Kirk would have loved for Stasi to have the freedom to travel there, at the same time, he appreciated the doctors' wisdom in holding her back.

"This is my way of helping."

"Wouldn't it be more effective if people knew you were

doing it? They might be inclined to give more." They came to the block near where they'd parked the helicopter.

Stasi stopped in her tracks.

It took Kirk just a second to pull his eyes away from the princess to see what she was looking at.

He quickly pulled her back behind the nearest building.

"What were those men doing near the helicopter?" Stasi asked.

"I don't know, but we can't stick around to find out. I think I recognize the one who was facing this way. He's Lydian."

"A member of the military?"

Kirk peeked around the corner of the building for a better look. "No, royal guard. And they've got guns."

"But members of the royal guard have no authority outside of Lydia."

"I don't believe this is an official visit. Those men are in tight with Viktor Bosch, and he's put a price on my head."

"They're not here to ensure our welfare," Stasi stated grimly.

"Hardly. Let's get out of here before they see us."

Kirk hurried up the street with Stasi keeping pace beside him. He didn't want to draw anyone's attention by running—not while there was still a chance they hadn't been seen. They needed to get away as quietly as possible. If it came to a fight, he'd only be injured worse.

Just as he'd begun to think they might have gotten away, two men leaped around the corner half a block in front of them, sprinting their way.

He looked back in time to see three more men pounding up the sidewalk behind them.

They were trapped.

# EIGHT

Stasi glanced to the right and the left. There didn't seem to be anywhere to hide.

Just ahead of them, a brightly painted red, double-decker tour bus had pulled away from the station, and was picking up speed as it headed out on the morning tour. She sprinted after it, wishing the slick, steep sides weren't quite so high. There didn't appear to be any way to vault up onto the open top.

Kirk pulled her around to the driver's side, where the bus itself blocked them from the view of the men who'd been chasing them. When he waved his arms, Stasi wondered what he was doing.

They didn't need to attract any more attention.

But then Stasi realized Kirk had pulled out a few of the bills she'd handed him, and was waving the money at the driver.

The door opened.

"Tell him to keep driving," Kirk requested of Stasi as they bounded aboard, and he shoved the cash at the smiling driver.

"He speaks English," the driver said of himself. "You want to go fast or slow?"

"Fast." Stasi glanced around and noted that the bus was still nearly empty at this early hour. Apparently, the driver had just set out in search of passengers, but he seemed content to carry just the two of them. Kirk had handed the man a much larger than usual fare.

The word had hardly left her lips than the bus accelerated.

*"Grazie!"* They both called as they headed for the stairs that led to the panoramic viewing deck.

"Stay down here," Kirk suggested before ascending the stairs.

Stasi waited below while Kirk cautiously proceeded above. Looking out the windows, she couldn't see the men who'd been chasing them, but that was little assurance. They'd appeared almost out of nowhere before.

Kirk descended with a cautious smile. "No sign of them, but I don't doubt they'll eventually guess what we did."

"They figured out about the helicopter quickly enough."

"I feared they might." Kirk's expression was grave. "Though I didn't think they'd find us on the ground so soon."

"They seem to be coordinated. And they apparently have plenty of resources at their disposal."

"I need to get you reunited with your parents." Kirk looked back in the direction of the hotel they'd been planning to check, though it had long before slipped from view. "You'll be safest with them."

"Will I?" Stasi settled into a seat and pulled Kirk into the seat beside her. "If my mother sent the jewels to me to keep them safe, my parents may be no better off than I am."

"I'll do what I can to protect you." Kirk slid down in the seat, and Stasi felt a twinge of surprise at how close he suddenly was. There wasn't any space between the seats, and almost nothing between their faces as they talked in muted whispers. "If that had come to a fight back there, I don't know what I would have done. You can't depend on me."

"You've managed quite well so far." As she spoke, the bus turned a corner, still traveling a clip faster than it was probably used to, and she found the centripetal force pushing her into Kirk. Her forehead pressed into his cheek, and she tried to right herself by pushing against him, but she didn't want to hurt his injured ribs, and so found herself fumbling at his shoulders.

He cleared his throat and put his hand on her arm, righting her as the bus straightened out. "Your Highness." His voice sounded dry.

Stasi met his eyes.

She'd been fighting the connection she felt to him for the last three days, always thinking whatever they were running from was far more urgent than whatever was between them.

But for the moment, they'd left what they were running from far behind.

And now there was nothing but what was between them.

"I have a name," she reminded him, feeling chafed that he insisted on using her title.

"If I use it—" Kirk's eyes never left her face "—it would put us on familiar terms."

"My forehead just smashed your cheek, Kirk. We *are* on familiar terms."

He pulled back, but only by a couple of inches. "You're a princess."

"Am I? Last I checked Lydia was crowning a new king in—" she glanced at the digital clock at the front of the bus "—a little over two hours. I think I'm just a very scared girl."

"A very wealthy girl," Kirk corrected, but somehow their faces had moved closer together again. She'd blame it on centripetal force, but she knew that wasn't the whole cause.

"I gave you half the money."

"I gave some of mine to the bus driver."

"I could give you more."

Kirk began to look away.

Stasi touched his hand. "We're equals. Actually, if you want to get down to it, you're my better. You're strong—"

"I'm injured."

"You're my elder."

"I'm not in your league. Your father wanted to marry you to a billionaire."

Stasi made a face. "Thank God you averted that disaster." She tried to remember what they'd been arguing about. Mostly she wanted him to stop talking and kiss her, but at the same time, she felt intimidated by the prospect. After all, she needed his help. What if a kiss changed everything between them?

"Anyway—" she cleared her throat "—you can call me Stasi."

"I need to get you back to your parents." Kirk had pulled back again. Perhaps he'd thought better of the kissing idea. Or perhaps a kiss had never crossed his mind at all.

Stasi took his cue. "They usually stay in the penthouse of that hotel back there. The staff knows them, and they have a secret entrance in back that leads straight to the elevators."

"Can you get us to that secret entrance?"

"I know the way, but it will depend on whether those men are still lingering around. Perhaps I should have had you park the helicopter elsewhere."

"That would only have left us with more ground to cover. No, we did what we thought was best. We simply underestimated the men who are after us."

Stasi settled back into her seat and tried not to let the ominous undertones of Kirk's words bother her. They'd underestimated the men before. It could easily happen again. "Do you think the bus driver would take us back around that way?"

"I suspect he'd take us anywhere—it just depends on the price." Kirk pulled out a couple of bills and headed to the front of the bus.

\* \* \*

Kirk asked the bus driver to let them out at an alley a block from the hotel. Fortunately, given their proximity to the bus stop, there were plenty of identical bright red, double-decker tourist buses swarming around. Even if their pursuers had figured out they'd hopped a bus, Kirk hoped they'd at least be confused about which one they might be on.

As they stepped down onto the cobbled path, Kirk glanced around and, seeing nothing, slipped a protective arm around Stasi's shoulders as they ducked up the alley toward the hotel.

A windowless steel door greeted them, and Stasi gave the handle a tug, smiling up at him as it opened. They stepped into a tiny foyer, where another, equally nondescript door barred their way. The side walls each held a door: one labeled *Cucina,* and the other *Domestica.*

The door in front of them was locked.

Stasi didn't look surprised. "There's a pass code, changed for every visitor. They give our family the same code every time we visit. If it works, that should tell us they're up there." She took a deep breath, but her fingers hovered over the buttons without pressing any of them.

Kirk leaned closer. "Do you remember the code?"

"Yes." Her voice squeaked, and she looked up at him with rapidly blinking eyes.

Since his arm was already draped protectively around her shoulders, Kirk pulled her closer against him. "It's all right."

"I know." She gulped. "The clock is ticking. I—I guess I'm just afraid. Why would they be here, hiding? Why would they leave me behind if they even suspected I'd survived? Surely they've seen on the news that Isabelle returned to Sardis. Why would they let her go alone?"

She trembled as he held her tight to his chest, and he wished he could calm the frantic beating of her heart.

"If you believe it may be dangerous, perhaps we shouldn't go?"

Stasi gave her head a tiny shake and clung to him. Kirk had never allowed himself to dream she would do such a thing, and guilty as he felt for thinking it, he felt honored that she would trust him enough to look to him for comfort.

But then, who else did she have? If she'd been reunited with her parents already, she'd be hugging them, not him. He had to get her back to them. It was his duty to keep her safe from every threat.

Kirk cleared his throat. "Your Highness?"

If she budged at all, it was only to burrow a little closer against his shoulder.

Unwilling to let their interlude continue, Kirk tried again. "Stasi?"

She looked up, and a minuscule smile bent the corners of her eyes. "So you do know my name."

"We need to keep moving. Either we try the door, or we need to seek safety far away from the men who are after us."

"The door." Stasi gulped a breath and punched a series of buttons, and they stepped through into a more lavishly appointed foyer, with a narrow set of stairs on one side and an elevator waiting with an open door on the other.

As they stepped into the elevator, Stasi pressed the button for the top floor. "None of the other elevators service the penthouse suites. Only those with the pass code can reach them."

The system made sense to Kirk, and he felt grateful for the added security it offered. Stasi would be safe with her parents there, and he could leave her behind with a clear conscience.

The elevator climbed rapidly, opening to an even more lavish landing, with a thick gold-and-cream rug, wide sparkling skylights, a hall table topped with an enormous vase of fresh flowers and two thick candlesticks that shone as though they were made of solid gold. Gilt-edged crown molding descended from the high ceilings until it met the arched molding above three doors.

Stasi turned to the door labeled with a gold *A*. "This is their favorite suite. It has a lovely view of the river." She approached and rapped the gold knocker.

Kirk hovered behind her, tense. Would the king and queen be inside? What would they think of his presence with their daughter?

He didn't have to wonder for long. Moments later, Queen Elaine opened the door herself, and Stasi threw herself into her mother's arms.

From somewhere in the suite, King Philip stepped out and approached his wife and daughter. The man's face looked drawn, almost sad. Well, that fit. Kirk figured the king and queen had been through plenty, with everything that had happened, and not knowing what had become of their daughter.

Kirk met the king's eyes. Philip took hold of the door. Stasi had followed her mother into the suite, sobbing and embracing happily. Kirk remained in the atrium, fairly certain he wasn't welcome inside. And yet, as King Philip held his gaze, the older man seemed intent on communicating something. Not animosity, though that would have made sense given their history. Not even thanks for returning his daughter safe and sound.

Whatever it was, Kirk didn't get a chance to figure it out before the door closed in front of him, cutting off his view of the royal family.

He hesitated in the atrium a moment longer. It was over. He'd done his job—delivered the princess into the safety of her parents' arms.

And yet, what had Philip been trying to tell him with his mournful eyes and half-open lips?

Kirk shrugged it off. He and the king would never see

eye to eye. That reality had been ingrained in his heart long ago. Stepping into the elevator, he punched the button for the ground floor and rode the car down, away from Stasi.

At the bottom, he stepped through the door with the code he didn't have to the tiny foyer with its three doors. Once he closed the door behind him there would be no coming back.

He grasped the handle resolutely and exited. The door closed behind him, and he stepped through the vestibule to the steel door that led outside, away from Stasi. There wasn't any reason for him to stay.

Except that he still had Stasi's cash in his pockets.

It was a great deal of money. He couldn't possibly keep it.

Kirk's fingers slid between the door and the jamb, stopping it from closing completely. As he was about to pull it open again, he heard one of the side doors opening.

He froze.

Though the narrow slit of open door, Kirk saw two men enter the foyer through the side door marked *Cucina.*

One man punched the pass code buttons, and the men stepped through toward the elevator. The elevator door opened, and as the men stepped inside, they turned to face him.

*No!* They weren't room service waiters at all, but the men who'd chased them from the helicopter. Kirk burst through the door and got his hand between the pass code door and its jamb an instant before it snapped shut. He pulled it open and slipped through just as the elevator door went completely closed.

He tried to jam his finger into the crack, to pry it open if he had to, but the illumined numbers above indicated the elevator had already begun to move.

They were headed straight for the princess.

Kirk dived for the stairs and vaulted the fire-code cement steps three at a time.

He had to reach Stasi and warn her.

He had to stop those men.

The throbbing spot near his lungs began to pinch.

There was no time for pain. If he failed to reach Stasi in time, anything might happen to her. The thought goaded him on, up flight after flight, until he'd lost count of the steps, and finally burst through at the top.

The door to the elevator was open.

So was the door to the A suite.

The men were nowhere in sight.

Stasi pulled back from her mother just enough to wipe her eyes. Her father had closed the door.

"Where's Kirk?" She cleared her throat and found her voice. Hadn't he followed her in?

Her father only shook his head. His eyes looked so sad, even sadder than they'd been after Thaddeus had disappeared.

Stasi tried to think. Her parents were alive! They were safe. It was what she'd been praying for, and yet, all she could think about was that Kirk had gone. And she hadn't even had the chance to tell her father how wonderful he'd been at protecting her.

"My baby." Queen Elaine smoothed Stasi's hair back from her cheeks. "I've been praying for you, for your safety."

Before the queen had quite finished speaking, Stasi heard a rap at the door.

Kirk!

Her heart leaped inside her. Of course, he'd been shut out by mistake. She crossed the room to open the door.

"Stasi." Her father stepped forward as if to stop her.

But she already had the door open.

Two rough-looking men stepped inside. One of them held a gun.

"Sorry to interrupt." The taller of the two spoke, while the shorter, stockier fellow kept his gun trained on both of them. Neither man looked sorry at all. The tall man sneered. "I need to claim something for my boss."

Stasi gasped. A hand clamped around her wrist.

Her father spoke from across the room. "Lucca, you can't—"

"They have every right, Philip." The voice behind her cut off the king. "The transfer is long overdue."

Stasi twisted around to see Corban Lucca, one of her father's three head generals, dressed in his customary uniform of the Lydian Navy. He pulled her toward the waiting men.

"No." Stasi dug her feet in. She didn't know the men. "I'm not going anywhere. Father?" Her father was king. Surely he could tell these men to stand down.

"I'm sorry, Stasi. I made deal. I thought it was the right choice."

As her father spoke, General Lucca dragged her across the marble floor toward the waiting men. Stasi tried to wrench her arm away, but the larger man was too strong for her, and his fingers only dug in that much more tightly as she fought him.

"You're hurting her!" Queen Elaine waved her arms as though torn between helping her daughter, and fear of making the situation worse. "Don't hurt her."

"Then she needs to come nicely." Lucca gave her arm another tug.

Suddenly the vase of flowers from the hall table flew into the room, sending water and fresh-cut blooms flying. The solid vase hit the shorter man in the head, knocking against him with a hollow thud, sending him crashing to the floor. His gun tumbled across the room, landing somewhere near the sofa.

Taking advantage of Lucca's momentary surprise, Stasi

lunged toward the doorway, escaping her captor for half a second before he grabbed her by the ankle.

She landed with a thump on the floor and kicked frantically, trying to free herself from Lucca's awful grasp.

The shorter man who'd held the gun was out cold on the floor, but the taller fellow who'd spoken wrestled with someone above her. When he went down in a slump, Stasi thought perhaps she might be able to get away after all.

Then boots thudded across the floor from one of the back bedrooms.

Stasi scrambled to her feet just in time to see a man throw a punch at Kirk. He ducked stiffly and tackled the man head-on.

Lucca let go of her ankle just long enough to grab her wrist but she stumbled forward, intent on reaching Kirk. She couldn't let him be hurt any worse.

Her mother was shouting from over by the couch. Her father tussled with another man who'd come from the bedroom. Kirk exchanged blows with the man near the door. Stasi struggled against Lucca's iron grip, and all the while her mother continued shouting.

A loud shot snapped them all to attention, and plaster rained down from the ornate ceiling. Stasi turned to see her mother holding the gun, still pointed at the ceiling.

"Stasi will go with Kirk." The queen gestured with the gun pointed toward Lucca.

She felt the man behind her hesitate, as though debating whether to call the queen's bluff. But the frantic look in the queen's eyes must have convinced him she wasn't stable enough to be messed with. She'd already pulled the trigger once, and her finger trembled against it still.

Lucca's grip relaxed, and Stasi tore away from him, securing her bag over her shoulder before wrapping her arms around Kirk and looking into his eyes, trying to determine how much pain he was in.

"Go!" Her mother gestured with the gun. "Go quickly."

"But the two of you must come with us," Stasi protested.

"I'm sorry." King Philip shook his head sadly. "Not this time."

Stasi gave her mother a pleading look, but the queen only shook her head, her expression firm. "Use the key," she told her daughter, then winked.

Kirk pulled her back into the hallway, and Stasi hurried after him, her thoughts conflicted. Everything had happened so quickly. She couldn't sort it out.

They stepped onto the elevator, and Kirk winced as he raised his arm to press the button for the ground floor.

Stasi pressed it for him, then let her fingers fall lightly on the spot where his rib had been cracked. "Is it worse?"

"I'm not sure. There's no time to look into it now. We need to get to the airport."

"The airport?" Stasi still hadn't absorbed the fact that they were leaving her parents behind. "Where are we going?"

"I don't know, but we obviously can't stay here. Those men could come after us again any second. What did your mother say to you?"

"'Use the key.'" Stasi repeated the cryptic words. "Do you think she means the pass code to the door? But that would only bring us right back to them."

"'Use the key,'" Kirk repeated. "Wasn't there a key inside the locket on the crown jewels?"

"Yes."

"What does it open?"

"My mother's journal." Stasi nodded resolutely. "You're right. We need to get to the airport. My mother mentioned to me just the other day that she'd left her journal at my grandparents' house. We need to catch the next flight to Atlanta."

# NINE

Kirk eased himself into the back of the taxi next to Stasi, who immediately swept her hands across his chest, obviously looking for the spot where his rib was cracked.

"It's all right for now. We don't have time to mess with it."

"The airport is at least a half an hour's drive from the hotel." Stasi shushed him.

Kirk caught her hand gently in his. "There's not enough room here to rebind me if you take the wraps off."

"Then I won't take them off." She slid her small hand between two of the buttons on his shirt. "Inhale as much as you can."

Since the woman seemed utterly determined, Kirk inhaled as ordered, and Stasi's fingers slipped under the bands. He felt a horrid pinch as she homed in on the tender spot at his rib.

"I don't think it's dislocated, even if it has broken in two," she determined, sliding her hand back out into the open. "You can exhale again."

Kirk allowed himself a few shallow breaths. "Your bindings held it in place. I'm glad for them."

"So am I." She sighed, and he could see all that had happened catching up to her, shining in the fear in her eyes. "What would I have done if you hadn't come back?"

"I was foolish to leave you without making certain the location was secure." Kirk had been kicking himself ever since he'd realized his mistake. But he'd been in such a hurry to part with her—before he did something foolish like act on his growing feelings—that he hadn't thought through the possible dangers. "I thought you'd be safe there. I was wrong."

"*I* was wrong to distrust you all those years. The more I learn, the more I'm convinced you did us all an enormous favor by helping my brother get away six years ago. My father was going to send me away with those terrible men."

"How do we know they're terrible?" Kirk had been trying to sort the good guys from the bad guys, but wasn't sure where to draw the line. "General Corban Lucca is the head of the entire Lydian Navy. He answers to your father."

"Apparently they've switched the pecking order around." Stasi's expression was grim. "Those men said they needed to claim something—me, apparently. And Lucca said the transfer was long overdue. I suppose that means I've been traded for something." Stasi bit her lip. "Do you think my parents will be safe there? I wish they would have come with us."

Kirk rubbed his face with his hands, thoughts of Stasi and King Philip and Prince Thaddeus all swirling about. Somehow they were all connected. And he was sure, if he could just sort out how they all came together, he might get at what was going on, and maybe even identify who their enemies were.

But in the meantime, he had a princess to reassure. "They looked unharmed. Distressed, but otherwise I don't think they've been injured. There were food wrappers at the kitchenette, so they've likely been fed."

"But what are they doing there? Why stay if they could get away?"

"I got the impression from what your father said that they felt by staying there, they were keeping you safe."

As he spoke, Stasi laid her hand on his shoulder, and her eyes went wide. "Listen," she whispered.

Kirk listened. The taxi driver had the radio on, tuned to someone talking in Italian. Probably a newscast. Whatever it was, Stasi began to smile.

"I don't speak Italian," he reminded her.

"The coronation has been postponed indefinitely. Valli has fallen under question. Isabelle is meeting with the United Nations. Oh, Kirk." Stasi threw her arms around his shoulders and pressed her face to his neck.

"Gentle," he reminded her, easing her back, though her actions didn't so much hurt his ribs as his heart, which thudded anxiously inside him.

She must have known the slight touch against his shoulders couldn't possibly be the source of his protest, because she leaned back just enough to look him in the eye. She looked guilty.

Had he hurt her feelings? "I just don't think we ought to be so close to each other."

Her wide blue eyes reminded him of a kitten who'd been caught getting into mischief. "I'm sorry. You're right. Where are my manners? I'm the one who's had all the social training."

"Don't apologize." Kirk felt even worse. "You were perfectly within the bounds of appropriate behavior."

"My behavior was unbecoming of my station." She looked utterly chastened.

Kirk's heart gave a lurch. He wanted to say something to erase the awkwardness he'd injected between them, but what was there? Nothing that wouldn't bring them right back together again. No, he needed to push her away. It was for the best.

He cleared his throat. "I have probably been sending inappropriate signals. We've gotten close these past few days."

He tried to clear his throat again, but something seemed to be stuck in it. "I'm the one who should apologize. And I'll do my best to keep an appropriate distance between us from now on."

"Oh." Stasi's mouth hung slightly open, and she looked a bit lost. Then she scooted back across the taxicab seat, putting more space between them. "I shall do the same." She gave him a small smile.

He nodded at her, unwilling to trust his voice again, and unsure what to say, anyway. They'd be at the airport soon, and surely both of them would need to rest on the flight. And once they arrived in Atlanta, Kirk was determined to make certain Stasi was safe before he left her again. But then he would leave her. He had to.

Stasi stared out the window at the clouds that floated past the plane, glad that they'd been able to purchase tickets for the earliest flight to Atlanta, and even more grateful that the first-class accommodations weren't full. They could talk, if they needed to, with little chance for anyone to overhear them.

But more than talk, she knew she ought to sleep on the ten-hour flight. She needed her rest—Kirk had reminded her of as much before settling back in the seat beside her—but she couldn't get her churning mind to slow down.

Had she been wrong to leave her parents behind? Would they be okay in Milan with General Lucca? And what were they involved in, anyway?

Even as she stewed over those thoughts, Stasi found herself thinking over and again about all that Kirk had done for her. She wanted to throw her arms around him and thank him, but he wouldn't let her.

Why not?

She let herself steal a look at Kirk as he rested. His face

had taken a few more blows in their latest skirmish, but the marks only served to highlight his ruggedness and soften her heart.

His eyes opened slightly. "Can't sleep?"

"I have too much on my mind," she confessed. "But don't let me wake you."

He sighed and sat up a little straighter. "I've just been resting my eyes. My mind is racing a hundred miles an hour."

"Have you reached any conclusions?"

"Just that I wish I'd listened more carefully to your brother. I fear it may be dangerous to try to contact him at this point," he whispered.

Though there wasn't anyone sitting near them, and the closest passengers appeared to be asleep, Stasi had learned the hard way not to trust anyone. She leaned a little closer to Kirk and spoke in a conspiratorial tone. "I was going to try to pick your brain about that. Do you think these events are connected to what happened six years ago?"

"I'm nearly certain of it. Your brother left because he said your father had made a deal with the devil, and Thad refused to be a part of it. He didn't go into details, and I didn't ask him for any."

It confirmed what Stasi had feared. "When those men arrived to take me away, Lucca said something like 'the transfer is long overdue.' I think he meant transferring me from the care of my parents, to whoever those men work for. I'm sure it's got to be related to the ambush on the motorcade, don't you think?"

"Somehow." Kirk nodded wearily. "I also think there's a reason why your mother sent the crown jewels to you. It was more important than sending you a message. She wanted to get them away from General Lucca."

"But why?" Stasi let out a long breath. "It's more complicated than I thought. What are we up against? Who are we fighting? And what are they after?"

"They're after the crown of Lydia, I'm almost certain of it." Kirk's lips thinned to a narrow line.

"But what do they want with me? I'm the *youngest*. Besides which, if Valli and his brothers wanted our father's throne, why are they keeping Dad alive? You'd think they'd get him out of the picture and step in and take it."

"There's got to be more to it than we can see."

Stasi closed her eyes and leaned back in her seat, overwhelmed. It was more than she could sort out. And yet, *someone* knew what was going on. She plucked up Kirk's hand that rested nearest her. "Pray," she whispered.

He raised an eyebrow, but a slow smile spread across his lips. "God knows what's going on," he said in a hope-filled tone. "Do you think He's going to explain everything to us?"

"Maybe not all at once, but the Psalms say, 'Your word is a lamp to my feet.' Sometimes God doesn't light the whole path, just the next step. If He can show us the next step, and then the step after that, eventually we will get it all sorted out."

"However it happens, it can't hurt to pray." Kirk eased himself a little closer to her, and bent his head in prayer.

Stasi poured her heart out to God and held tight to Kirk's hand. She prayed for guidance and protection and wisdom, and toward the end of her prayer, she prayed for Kirk. "Lord, I know I don't deserve Kirk's friendship. I was so cruel to him for so many years. You've seen fit to help me through him, and I'm forever grateful. Bless him for all he has done for me, and heal his injuries."

The words came from her heart, and she didn't expect them to be reciprocated. But in the next breath, she heard Kirk praying for her. "Thank You, God, for entrusting the princess into my care. Help me to protect her, from any and every threat. Thank You for making her a talented, delightful person. Amen."

Though Kirk had ended the prayer, Stasi kept her head bowed and her eyes pinched tight shut as the meaning of Kirk's words sunk in. When she dared to open her eyes, she found him watching her.

"I haven't offended you, have I?" Sincere concern shone on his face.

"My talents?" Her voice was raspy, her throat dry. She might have attributed it to the dry air on the plane, but she knew in her heart there was more to it.

"Your jewelry—I don't know much about it, but obviously the savvy shoppers of Milan know beauty when they see it."

Stasi blinked rapidly. "You think I should put my name on my jewelry line?"

"Wouldn't it sell better with your name on it? And by letting people know that you're supporting your sister's mission trips, you'd be raising awareness for her cause. Does *she* even know that you're supporting her?"

"No," Stasi confessed. "I've always done it anonymously."

"There's something to be said for anonymous giving," Kirk conceded. "But in your case, given the circumstances, I think your efforts would be more effective if you used your name."

"Possibly." Stasi sighed. "But that's the least of my concerns. You're assuming we'll get through all this."

"Didn't we just pray that we would?"

"True. But there's still so much we need to sort out. I don't know who to believe or who to trust anymore."

Kirk looked at her with sadness simmering in his hazel eyes.

She squeezed his hand. "Except for you. I trust you."

"Thank you." He settled back into his seat with a weary smile. "You need your rest."

* * *

Stasi felt grateful that Kirk was able to rent a car in Atlanta using one of his credit cards.

"I just hope nobody's tracing my activity," he murmured in her ear after swiping the card.

"There's a chance they might have been watching us at the airport," Stasi reminded him. "If they saw what flight we took, your credit card isn't going to tell them anything they don't already know. But this is supposed to be the world's busiest airport. Even if they trace us here, it should take them a while to track us down."

"I hope to be gone by then."

Kirk insisted on carrying Stasi's bags to the car.

"You're injured. I can carry my own bag," she protested.

"I'm not on my deathbed." He also insisted on driving. "I know the way to Porterdale. My grandparents live near there, too," Kirk reminded her as he pulled out of the parking lot. "Both of my parents went to school with your mother growing up."

"That's right." Stasi observed the way he took all the correct turns without being told. "I suppose you grew up visiting down here, too."

"On occasion. More during my teenage years."

"I wonder why we didn't travel together, then? Or get together when we were down here?"

Kirk cleared his throat. "My grandparents weren't always happy about the situation, with my parents living in Lydia, and all of that."

"Why not?" It was the first Stasi had ever heard anything about Kirk's grandparents. The idea that they might not be thrilled with Albert and Theresa's choices intrigued her. "Lydia is a fine place to live. And your parents have very high positions at the royal palace. They ought to be proud of them."

"It's nothing against Lydia."

"What is it, then?"

Kirk scowled at the road, and for a long moment, Stasi thought he wasn't going to say any more. But once he'd merged onto Interstate 20, he cleared his throat. "Have you heard of the Covington Textile Company?"

"I've seen their signs in the area. Are they related to you? I always assumed they were named after the town of Covington." She stifled a gasp. "Is the town of Covington named after your family?"

"According to the official town record, it's named after the Brigadier General Leonard Covington, but I don't know when he was ever there. My ancestors settled in the area long before the town was incorporated, but some folks don't want to believe they have any stake in the place."

"You think the story about the general was invented? But who would start such a rumor?"

"My mother's family." Kirk kept his eyes on the road.

From what little Stasi could see of his profile view, he looked sad. "I don't understand."

"It's a long story."

"We have time."

Kirk gave her a resigned look. "My father's ancestors started the Covington Textile Company. They got along fine until my great-grandfather took over as a young man. He was a drunk and would have run the company into the ground had it not been for my mother's grandfather. He was their manager. He ran the place, built it up into a fine success, and eventually bought the whole company, even keeping the name, but telling everyone it was named after the town, which was named after the general.

"My great-grandfather claimed he was cheated, that his manager embezzled the money that was used to buy the company out from under him."

"Was there any truth to that?"

"If there was, the evidence is long gone."

"So your father's family didn't like your mother's family."

"Nor vice versa. After the buyout, the Covingtons lived in poverty. They tried to get back on their feet, even talked about taking the company back, but most of them had trouble with alcohol and the law. My mother's family looked down their noses at them.

"Then my father came along. He was an honor student, and was headed to college to study business. Folks began to say he was determined to take the family business back."

"Was your mother's family scared?"

"Not until their daughter started dating him. When they found out, they refused to let her see him, and sent her on an all-expense-paid trip to Europe for a year, with her best friend to keep her company."

"My mother." Stasi smiled. She knew this part of the story. "Theresa and my mom visited Lydia, and my mom caught the eye of the young Lydian Prince. And they all lived happily—" Her voice caught. "Well, they lived happily ever after, until lately." She shook her head. "So how did your parents get together after all that?"

"Mom came back to Georgia and found she and Dad were still in love. They wanted to run away together, so Elaine invited them to come to Lydia and work at the palace. It took their families a long time to forgive them—not until my grandfather nearly died of a heart attack, and decided he wanted to meet me after all. They tolerate me, but my parents still don't come home very often."

"It's terribly sad," Stasi concluded. "And yet, if they hadn't been through all that, I wouldn't be a princess." She stared out the window as they neared the town of Covington, where they'd turn off to rural Porterdale, where her grandparents lived. She caught her reflection in the window and bit her lower lip, wishing her father would have abdicated and run off with her mother, instead of her mother leaving Georgia to become a queen.

What would it have been like to grow up in this town? Would she still have known Kirk? If she wasn't a princess, she wouldn't have to worry about the coup that was trying to overthrow her father's government.

A sorrowful yearning took hold of her heart as she watched the countryside flash by with her reflection in the window superimposed on everything she saw, stamping her impression as though she belonged there. What would it be like to be a regular Georgia girl, as her mother had once been?

She stole a glance at Kirk. If she wasn't a princess, perhaps he wouldn't be so insistent on keeping a proper distance between them. Longing settled over her—for love and peace and a simpler way of life. Would she rather have Kirk than all the jewels of Lydia?

The idea stole her breath. Maybe she didn't want to be a princess anymore, after all.

# TEN

Kirk was surprised by the house Stasi led him to—a ram-shackle farmhouse with several barns in various states of falling down. Granted, Kirk had always heard that Queen Elaine came from humble roots, but he hadn't realized how rustic her childhood home had been. Though the Watkinses' farm had its own charm, unlike the royal palace in Lydia, there was nothing extravagant about it.

The yard overflowed with all manner of flowers and animals: chickens, cats, bossy geese that honked and waddled after their car all the way up the drive, and a yellow three-legged mutt who limped over and sniffed Kirk's hand curiously when he got out of the car.

"Isn't it glorious?" Stasi's eyes twinkled as she stretched from the car ride. "Look at Gramma's roses." She sighed at the enormous climbing blooms that appeared to have nearly swallowed up the house.

"They're beautiful, but I'm a bit surprised—I'd think the parents of a queen would live in luxury."

"Mother has begged them to let her move them, or fix up the place, but they refuse to change anything. It's part of who they are, and also their opportunity to allow us to live like normal people whenever we came to visit them. Besides—" she smiled at him knowingly "—I believe my mother has made the same offer to your parents, but they insist on staying in that tiny cottage. It's the same thing."

A screen door opened with a squeal of hinges and a heavy-set woman in an apron and calico dress eased herself down the cement stairs. "Stasi?"

"Gramma!" Stasi flew at the woman and tackled her in a hug.

"Oh, my little princess! You're alive! You're not hurt? Why didn't you let us know you were coming to visit?"

"I'm sorry, Gramma. I couldn't risk calling. Where's Grampa?"

"He's inside trying to get that computer of his to tell him news about you. He's gotten all of half a minute's footage of your sister. She's testifying before the United Nations. Darrel!" She hollered back through the screen door. "Stasi's here!"

"Little princess!" A man in overalls appeared and scooped up Stasi in a bear hug. "How did you get here? How did you make it through all that?"

Kirk watched, unsure how to proceed, and more than a little surprised to find the royal princess's mother came from such a humble background—and Stasi apparently loved everything about it.

"This is Kirk." Stasi pulled him into their circle. "He rescued me. I wouldn't be here if it wasn't for him. I wouldn't even be alive."

"You'd have made it all right—" Kirk began, but the words were squeezed out of him by her grateful grandparents, and Stasi had to caution them to be careful of his ribs.

While Stasi traded more hugs and news that her parents were indeed alive, the Watkinses led them inside, past piles of books and bags of cat food, plants perched in precariously tilted pots atop a jumble of furniture, and on every available wall, pictures of family. Snapshots of Stasi and her siblings hung side by side with pictures of what had to be cousins, posing with ponies and smiling from school pictures with gap-toothed grins.

"Gramma's making strawberry jam." Darrel Watkins explained as he led them through a steam-filled kitchen where four pots bubbled gooey red on the stove.

"It smells divine." Stasi breathed deeply as they passed through.

"I'll cook us up some pancakes later. We'll pour the soft jam on like syrup."

They filed through to a living room where colorful knitted afghans covered aging furniture. "Have a seat." Darrel lowered himself into a desk chair in front of a sleek computer, which looked out of place amid the homey clutter. "Now, what brings you halfway across the globe?"

"I've come for mother's journal. She told me she left it here on her last visit."

"Ah." Her grandfather shuffled under a stack of magazines and papers, then held out a silver notebook-size hard case. "Is this what you're looking for?"

"Yes, that's it. Thank you." Stasi reached for the locked case. "I'm surprised she left it behind here. She's very protective of it."

"Funny thing about that." Her gramma bustled about, fluffing pillows and clearing away books to make space for everyone to sit. "We didn't even know it was here until Grampa found it under a pile of books. She must have hid it under there."

"You're sure things didn't get placed on top of it by accident?"

"Not possible." Her grandfather shook his head solemnly. "This may look like a room in disarray to you, but I know when I've touched each of these piles. These are strata of research. Her journal was among things I haven't moved in six months. No one had touched that pile."

Stasi felt the hairs rise on the back on her neck. She knew her grandfather was quite particular about his peculiar organization methods. The man was quirky, but brilliant. Thad had inherited his knack for inventions from him.

Stasi turned the metal case over in her hands. "Do you think she left it for you to find?"

"Yes." Her grandfather met her eyes. "The question is why?"

The lock on the back of the case held a tiny keyhole. Stasi squinted at the miniscule engraving under the lock: Mt 16:19.

"Do you have a Bible?" she asked her grandparents.

"Of course." Her grandmother laughed. "Which version would you like?" Lois Watkins climbed onto a stool to reach a high shelf and handed down a leather-clad volume to Kirk.

"Matthew chapter sixteen, verse nineteen," she requested.

He flipped through the pages and read. "'I will give you the keys of the kingdom of heaven. Whatever you bind on earth will be bound in heaven, and whatever you loose on earth will be loosed in heaven.'" He looked up and met her eyes. "What does it mean?"

Stasi had toted her carry-on bag in over her shoulder, and now rummaged around in the small duffel until she found the securely wrapped package that held the crown jewels. She'd left her sapphire set with Giovanni, but thankfully, hadn't wanted to leave the crown jewels in the same city her mother had gone to so much trouble to mail them from, so they'd been safely stowed away in her bag the whole time.

She turned over the central stone of the necklace and clicked open the hidden locket on the back plate. When she lifted out the tiny key, engraved letters stared back at her: Mt 16:19.

Stasi fumbled with the key and nearly dropped it.

Kirk's steady hand covered hers. "Are you okay?"

"It's the same verse." She showed him, and pinched her eyes shut. Though she knew the key would open the journal, the echoing verses touched a vulnerable spot on her heart. If her mother had left the book behind on her last trip months before, she must have known even then that something was afoot. Stasi pressed the key into Kirk's hand. "Can you do it?" Her fingers shook so much, she was afraid she might drop the key and lose it amid the clutter of her grandparents' house.

With a solemn look, Kirk took the key and undid the lock, opening the hard-bound book to reveal pages and pages of her mother's handwriting.

Stasi bit her lip and looked up.

"I'd best tend to the jam," her grandmother said, shuffling off toward the kitchen. "And don't you worry about helping me with the pancakes. Looks like you've got reading to do."

Her grandfather stood as well, and addressed Kirk. "How about I give you the nickel tour?"

"Sure." Kirk followed him through the room, but paused as he passed by Stasi's chair. His gentle hand touched her shoulder. "Are you going to be okay?"

Stasi tried to give him her most reassuring smile. "I hope so. Don't go too far, okay?"

The pancakes and strawberry syrup tasted delicious, but Kirk couldn't get over the haunted look in Stasi's eyes. She'd told her grandparents bits and pieces of their adventures, but no one asked about the contents of the journal, and Stasi didn't bring it up. He could tell from the bookmark partway into the volume that she hadn't finished reading yet.

Kirk helped the Watkinses with the dinner dishes and a few chores around their small farm. The place made him chuckle—stubbornly unchanged from the way it had been when they'd raised their seven children, except for a few outstanding expensive items that Queen Elaine had given them as gifts—including the computer in their living room, and an Aston Martin convertible they kept parked in one of the barns.

"I prefer to drive my truck." Darrel Watkins pointed to a rusty Chevy parked near the house. "But I take this little buggy around the pasture every week or two, just to keep her running good."

The high-performance vehicle looked as though it had been neatly polished recently, save for a trail of dusty paw prints that scampered across the hood. Kirk tried not to cringe.

After his tour of the farm, Kirk returned to find Stasi hugging her knees in a corner of the sofa, her mother's journal inches from her nose. "How's it going?"

"Awful." She put the book down and motioned for him to sit beside her.

"Have you finished reading it?"

"Not quite, but I'm not sure I want to." Tired lines under her eyes made her look older. She leaned toward him and rested her chin on his shoulder. "I don't want to know the things I know. When Thaddeus said our father made a deal with the devil, he wasn't kidding."

"Who's the devil?"

Stasi shrugged. "Mom only refers to him with a number, 8."

"So what's the deal?"

"I don't think Dad ever explained it all to Mom, but I get the impression Dad was selling the crown."

"Auctioning the royal jewels?"

"If only. His royal authority, all his power—it's not clear whether he sold them straight out, or if they were held in lien against a debt."

"And the debt?"

"I don't know. If it's a monetary amount, it's got to be a big one. Maybe the whole national debt."

"I didn't realize Lydia had a national debt."

"Neither did I." Stasi lifted her head from his shoulder, and Kirk immediately missed her. But she picked up his hands instead. A tear slipped from her cheek.

Kirk instinctively reached up and wiped it away. "Hey, now," he soothed, "don't lose hope. I don't think your mom left that book here just to depress you. She gave you the key for a reason."

"What reason?"

"Because she thought you could help?" Kirk wasn't sure of his answer, but it seemed to be the only thing that fit.

"So, my dad spent the last six or more years selling the country to the devil, and now I'm supposed to fix it all by myself?"

"Not by yourself."

"It's too big." Stasi shook her head. "I don't want to be a princess anymore, Kirk. If our parents had never gone to Lydia, you and I would just be two regular folks. Can't we just hide out here? Can't we just be normal people?"

A strange, swirling hope began in the pit of Kirk's stomach. If Stasi wasn't a princess anymore, then she wouldn't be off-limits to him. "But we can't just leave your family in the lurch. What would happen to your parents and siblings? What would become of Lydia?"

Stasi had inched herself closer as they'd talked, and now she perched on the couch, leaning so close to him they were nearly nose to nose. "If we can get this sorted, will you help me run away?"

She was too close, her strawberry-scented breath too sweet. His heart thumped out a deafening plea in his ears. "What do you mean?"

"You helped Thad run away. Can't you take me somewhere?"

"Take you and leave you?"

"Come with me."

"Run away with you?"

"Your parents ran away together."

Her offer hung in the air between them, like temptation dangled on a hook. Kirk thought of a million protests. His parents' decision to run away and get married had torn their families apart. And he'd gone on trial for murder for helping her brother leave. "Stasi, you're not suggesting—"

The look in her eyes changed to one of longing. It took him less than a second to guess what she was about to do, leaving him another three seconds to try to stop her.

He didn't try to stop her.

Her lips brushed against his tentatively, then pulled closer in a heady swirl of emotion. He'd dreamed of kissing her, but no dream could match the reality of what he felt in that moment. All the feelings he'd tried to deny for so long could no longer be ignored, and everything he'd tried to convince himself she couldn't possibly feel, she convinced him she most certainly felt.

"Stasi." He cupped her cheek in his hand, warring between drawing her closer and pushing her away. He could have kissed her forever, but he knew it wouldn't stay just a kiss.

He pulled back. "Stasi, we can't. I can't. You're a princess."

"Why not?"

"I don't think running away from a problem makes it go away. It only makes it worse."

Stasi deflated back, away from him, her expression sorrowful. "I suppose you're right."

As the cool air passed between them, Kirk found himself immediately missing her. Was he right? He wasn't entirely convinced he was.

\* \* \*

After the last page, Stasi closed the journal with a sigh and went to find Kirk. He'd slunk off after their kiss, but she'd heard him go out the back door, and never heard him return.

She found him sitting at the picnic table, watching the sunset color the sky in a palate of pink, purple and orange.

"Where are Gramma and Grampa?"

"They headed to the grocery store. I think we drank up the last of their milk at supper."

"Oh." Stasi felt a twinge of guilt, but in the scope of everything else she was dealing with, running out of milk was nothing. "I finished the journal."

"Learn anything?"

"I think I know why my room was broken into."

Kirk sat up straight. "Why?"

"The same reason my mother sent me the crown jewels. Someone *was* looking for something. A piece is missing from the crown jewels—has been for years. Eight wants it."

"What is it?"

"Have you ever heard of the scepter of Charlemagne?"

A strange look crossed over Kirk's face. "Why?"

"Ever since the days of Charlemagne, every ruler of Lydia has, as a part of his or her coronation, signed their name to the charter that is stored inside the scepter. If they don't possess the scepter, their rule isn't valid."

"So, whoever has the scepter..."

"Whoever has the scepter could conceivably determine who becomes the next rightful ruler. And this whole mess in Parliament, trying to sort out which is the rightful reigning line, could be determined by looking at the charter. If my father or his father didn't sign it, for any reason, their reigns could be deemed invalid. That would strengthen the case for Basil's line, and Valli or one of his brothers could be crowned."

"So, no one knows where the scepter is?"

"No. The kings have always kept it hidden. But, according to mother's journal, my father doesn't have it anymore."

Kirk let out a long, slow sigh. "Do you know what it looks like?"

"I saw it at my father's coronation, after my grandfather died."

"Is it about this long?" He held out his hands half a meter apart.

"Yes."

"All inlaid with gold and silver and amethysts, with a small replica of your father's crown on top, topped with a cross?"

Stasi's heart hammered inside her as Kirk described the item perfectly. "Yes."

With his elbows planted on his knees and his back bent low, Kirk hung his head, for a long time avoiding looking at her.

"How do you know what it looks like?" she asked him finally.

"Your brother showed it to me."

"Where? When?"

"Six years ago. Thad took it with him when he ran away."

"So where is it now?"

"I'm not sure. He might still have it with him. Or it might be hidden somewhere on Dorsi."

Stasi fairly panted. "Can we call him and ask where—"

"We can't risk it," Kirk cut her off with finality. "We cannot mention it aloud, certainly not over the phone. Wherever he hid it, you can be certain it's safe. If we go messing around, we could give away the hiding place. No, it's only safe as long as we never speak of it again."

"Then what can we do?"

"Did your mother's journal tell you anything else?"

"At the very end, after the regular entries, she jotted a

phone number. Judging by the area code it's in New York City."

"Just the number—nothing to identify it?"

"It was accompanied by one word. *Sanctuary.*"

For a long time, Kirk mulled her revelation in silence. "What do you suppose it's for?"

"I don't know. Mother left the journal here six months ago. The phone number may be years old. It could be anything." She yawned, deep exhaustion catching up with her in spite of the rapid beating of her heart. "For now, I need my sleep. We both do."

Her grandparents had plenty of guest rooms, and had shown Stasi and Kirk where they would be staying on opposite ends of the house. Wishing Kirk a good night, Stasi headed for bed, and hoped the new day would bring new answers.

Stasi slept hard, and awoke early the next morning to the sound of the ringing phone. She could hear her grandmother answer the call.

There was a pause, and then her grandmother shouted, "Elaine! Elaine!"

Leaping from the bed, Stasi grabbed the robe that hung from the hook on the back of the bedroom door, threw it on, and ran to where her grandmother stood by the phone, a frantic expression on her face.

"Gramma? What was it?"

"That was your mother on the phone," Lois Watkins explained as Kirk ran out from his room in a too-small robe. "She didn't introduce herself, but I recognized her voice."

"What did she say?"

"They traced Kirk's credit card to the rental car. You've got less than a half an hour. Run. They're on their way."

"Who? They're coming here?"

"I don't know. That's all she said. I would guess they'd be coming here."

"We have less than half an hour?" Stasi looked around frantically. She'd showered the night before. But she needed to dress, and they needed to plan. "What are we going to do?"

# ELEVEN

"You can drive the Aston," Darrel Watkins offered, shoving a set of keys at Kirk.

"That's a generous offer—" Kirk began, hesitant to borrow the expensive vehicle.

"It's not an offer. You're taking it and you're leaving in the next five minutes. You got that?"

"Yes, sir."

"I'll take that rental car of yours into Covington. The rental company has an office there."

"No, Grampa, it's too dangerous," Stasi objected.

Darrel dismissed his granddaughter's concerns with a wave. "Bah! Nothing to it. Your gramma can follow in the truck and pick me up. And if anyone *does* try to follow us, I'll lead them on a wild-goose chase."

Kirk wanted to object, as well, and insist that Darrel and Lois would be safer hiding out at home, but he wasn't convinced they would be, not if their pursuers were on their way to the farm.

Stasi must have reached the same conclusion. "I can't believe I've sucked you into this. It's all my fault—I should never have come."

"Don't be silly!" Lois Watkins squeezed Stasi in a hug. "I'm so glad you came here, even if it was for a short visit.

Your grandfather and I were worried sick, but now we know that God kept you safe. I believe He'll continue to keep you safe. But you've got to get going."

"But I—" Stasi shook her head, continuing to protest.

"We'll be all right," her grandmother assured them both. "God is still in charge. What's the worst that can happen?" She lifted her gaze heavenward.

"Gramma, do be careful."

"We will." Her grandmother gave her another hug. "But bear in mind—there's nothing more important than our faith. If we keep tight hold of that, no enemy can touch us. Not really."

Kirk took Stasi's grandmother's words to heart as he carried their bags toward the Aston Martin. He understood what Lois was getting at—that even if they died, they went to be with God. It was a promise he looked forward to—in sixty or seventy years. Unfortunately, the enemies who were after them seemed intent on accelerating the process.

Stasi clicked the trunk release button, and a flurry of leaves swirled around the open bay of the barn.

"Oh, Darrel." Lois clucked her tongue disapprovingly at the sight of the trunk packed full of dry brown leaves. "You never did anything with those leaves."

"Let me get my leaf blower. I can have them cleared out in two minutes."

Stasi shook her head. "I'm not sure we have two minutes to spare. We can put the bags in the backseat."

Kirk obediently tucked their bags into the tiny backseat and hopped behind the wheel.

"Be careful," Lois called as they drove off with the windows down.

"You, too! I love you!" Stasi waved until they turned the corner at the end of the driveway.

Kirk quickly steered them toward I-20, praying they'd

somehow make it to the airport undetected. The Tuesday-morning traffic into the city was already growing heavy, but fortunately the cars were still moving at a brisk clip.

"Are we taking I-285 to the airport?" Stasi asked.

"It's the most obvious route." Kirk had been mulling over the same question. "Do we want to take the most obvious route?"

"I suppose that depends on whether we think they'll catch up to us. They don't know what we're driving."

"We hope they don't know what we're driving," Kirk corrected her. "We're not even sure who we're up against, or the scope of their knowledge or resources."

"Do you think they might know my mother gave Grampa this car?"

"It's not out of the realm of consideration." He kept up with traffic, taking care to drive only as fast as the other cars around them. There was no point drawing extra attention. "If we don't think we're being followed, we can take I-285, but if I suspect they're following us before then, I'll take another route. Fortunately, I learned the ins and outs of Atlanta from visiting my grandparents. Hopefully our pursuers don't have that advantage."

They drove in silence a short time longer, and Kirk kept his eyes on the road, ever alert for anything out of the ordinary. As promised, he took I-285, and they approached the airport without incident.

"We're almost there." Stasi's hands had been clenched tight in prayer for the whole drive. "We just might make it."

Kirk barely heard her words. He'd been watching a black sedan in his rearview mirror as it swerved quickly through traffic, rapidly gaining on them. He'd hoped it was an emergency vehicle, or some other innocent, unrelated speeding car. But as it came up closer, it ducked into their lane right behind them and slowed down to follow them.

"Hold on!" Kirk instructed Stasi as he skipped from his airport-bound lane across to the outer lanes.

"Where are you going?"

"The I-75 exit." They'd almost reached the spot, but two full lanes of traffic flowed between them.

"You'll never make it!"

With another quick glance in his mirror, Kirk caught an opening and took it, making it across both lanes smoothly and hopping on the exit. As he merged into the traffic, he glanced back. "Did we lose them?"

Blaring horns behind them indicated their pursuers had upset the other drivers.

"They made it," Stasi moaned. "It wasn't pretty, but they made it. Now what?" Stasi asked as they tore down I-75 into the city, away from the airport. The morning commuter traffic nearly choked the road, slowing them down somewhat. Fortunately, it also put a few cars between them and their pursuers.

Two more exits slid by them, and Kirk stayed in the outer lane as though preparing to exit. "If I could take Langford Parkway to the Lakewood Park district without them following me, they wouldn't get another chance to exit for two miles. With the way the incoming traffic is choking up, that might buy us the time we need to circle back to the airport. But how am I going to exit without them seeing me?"

Stasi thought quickly. "Get over another lane. Act like you're not going to exit."

Kirk hesitated only a second before obeying. "The exit's coming up," he reminded her.

"The car beside us has his blinker on. When he takes the exit, you swerve in after him. Then pop the trunk."

As quickly as Stasi explained what to do, Kirk did exactly that, sending an explosion of leaves scattering everywhere behind them just as they left the roadway behind.

Cars honked, but the traffic had already been slowing to a crawl. Stasi braced herself, but she heard no crash of metal, only a few squealing brakes. Good. She didn't want to cause an accident.

"Can you see them?"

Stasi looked back, but the open trunk and swirling leaves blocked her view. Then she spotted the black sedan moving past the exit, still in the wrong lane, but slowing down as the morning commuters jammed the road.

"They're up there. And they're not going anywhere for a while."

"Good." Kirk took the first opportunity to turn around, closed the trunk, and then hopped back on the Interstate, this time taking I-285 south toward the airport. "Let's hope that was their only car."

They arrived at the airport, grabbed their bags and hurried to find a ticket kiosk. Stasi prayed the whole time that their pursuers would stay stuck in traffic for as long as it took them to board a plane to New York.

Kirk had never been a fan of big cities. Though he'd spent most of his life in Lydia's capital city of Sardis, the most populous town in the kingdom was home to only a few hundred thousand people. It was a far cry from the busiest airport in America, where the crowds seemed to swarm in droves. And since he knew their pursuers had to have guessed where they were headed, the Atlanta airport felt far from safe.

He and the princess hurried inside along with the rest of the morning crowd, and Kirk struggled to get his bearings. True, he'd flown into the airport many times over the years. But he'd never felt at home there.

Fortunately, the busiest airport in America had plenty of available seats for Tuesday-morning flights to New York City. After securing a flight, Stasi suggested they call the number she'd found in her mother's journal, in hopes that whoever was on the other end would really be able to offer them sanctuary.

Kirk kept a close eye on Stasi as he dialed the number with his cell phone. It rang five times before a machine picked up.

*"You have reached the private line of Nicolas Grenaldo, the president of Sanctuary International. I'm either on the phone or away from my desk. You're welcome to leave me a message. If this is an emergency, or you are in need of assistance, please call any of the following numbers."*

"I need to write," Kirk whispered hastily to Stasi, motioning with his hand for pen and paper. She dug around in her bag and pulled out a pen, then stuck out her arm.

He raised a questioning eyebrow.

"I don't have any paper. Just write on my hand."

Kirk cringed at the thought of defacing her royal person, but the mechanically captured voice was already relaying the numbers, and Stasi gave him one of her royal commanding looks that seemed to expect compliance. He jotted the numbers across the inside of her palm.

"What are they?" she asked as he closed the call.

"Phone numbers." He explained what the voice mail greeting had told him. "Have you ever heard of Sanctuary International?"

"It sounds distantly familiar. I don't know if I've heard of it before, or if I recognize the word because of the notation in my mother's journal. And anyway, what else have we got to go on? Should we call one of these numbers?"

"I'll call all of them if that's what it takes."

He tried the first two numbers and reached only voice mail. "Whatever kind of organization this is, they don't tend to be very responsive," he grumbled, holding Stasi's hand so he could see the next number. Her arm tensed.

"What is it?"

She motioned with her eyes, but kept her face schooled in a natural expression. "By the water fountain. He's been watching us."

Kirk didn't recognize anything about the man until he reached up and tugged at something near his ear. Not only did Kirk quickly realize the man was using a device at his ear to communicate with someone else in the airport, but he recognized him as someone he'd seen before in uniform. "It's another one of Bosch's men. I think we should get going."

They gathered their bags with deliberate nonchalance and headed hand in hand through the airport.

"Where are we going?" Stasi asked. "We don't want to miss our flight, but we don't want to lead them right to it, either."

Much as Kirk hated to admit it, he had to confess, "I don't know. There are plenty of people here, maybe we can lose them. We should exchange some of our euros for American dollars." He spoke under his breath as they weaved through the foot traffic, his eyes straight ahead, his grip firm on her hand.

"I saw a sign for currency exchange. There tends to be extra security there."

Kirk swallowed. He was in over his head. "Let's try to find the exchange, then. Maybe we'll lose them on the way."

"This way." Stasi tugged him along, and Kirk scoured the faces that swept past them. He hadn't realized Viktor Bosch had such a long arm. It surprised him that the head of the royal guard could reach them halfway around the globe. Most likely he was working with someone else. Someone powerful, with international connections.

It didn't bode well for their odds of escaping.

With relief, he spotted the sign for the currency exchange and took his place in line. Though he hadn't dared look behind them while they were walking, now that they'd stopped, he pulled the princess close and looked past her head.

"See anyone?" she asked.

"Not yet." Kirk let out an uneasy breath. "I'm going to keep dialing while we wait. We need to know what we're getting into before we get to New York."

"Need my arm?" Stasi offered.

"I'll try the first number again."

Kirk dialed the number from memory, once again with no result. He sighed as Stasi reached the front of the line and exchanged a couple of large stacks of their euros for American dollars.

As soon as Stasi had their money exchanged, she pulled him out of the way of the next person in line. "Now what?"

"I don't know. I'm not getting an answer."

"It doesn't matter. We need to hurry if we're going to catch our flight to New York. You can try calling again right before we board. If it's someone we can trust, they can have a car waiting for us at the airport."

Kirk nodded. It was a good enough plan, except for the question neither one of them spoke aloud, though he was certain the princess was well aware of it. What would they do if it wasn't someone they could trust?

Constantly alert for the reappearance of Viktor's man, Kirk paced by the windows, watching their plane taxi over to receive the passengers. They'd be boarding soon.

Stasi gave him a studied look. They'd both been watching for the man while they'd bought a quick lunch, but so far had seen nothing. Where had the man gone? It didn't seem likely that he'd given up. More likely, he'd gathered reinforcements.

The flight attendant called to begin preboarding passengers who needed assistance. It was only a matter of time.

"It's now or never," Stasi whispered to him.

Kirk said a final silent prayer and dialed the first number

again. He nearly jumped when a brusque voice answered on the first ring. The man jumped into the conversation without saying hello.

"Have you found the princess?"

Unsure who he was talking to or what they knew of the situation, Kirk took a second to answer. "She's with me."

"Impossible! I'm surprised you've made it there. They didn't give you much of a fight, then?"

"We've had our hands full," Kirk acknowledged, trying to think how the man on the other end of the line knew so much about the situation. "Is this the president of Sanctuary International?"

"Of course it is. Who are you?"

Kirk faltered. What should he say?

"Say, who is this, anyway? Have you got the princess of Lydia?"

Kirk's heart hammered in his chest. *Lord, give me wisdom.* "I do."

"Where have you got her?"

"We're on our way to JFK Airport."

The man whistled long and low. "What's it going to take for us to get her back?"

Kirk could hear himself panting into the phone, and he felt distracted by what was happening around him. The flight attendant called for their seats. Stasi tugged him toward the line to board.

He followed her lead, and the tugging in his heart prompted him on. "Send a car." He quickly made arrangements to meet the vehicle at the New York airport. He was to call again for the car five minutes before they were ready to walk out of the airport. Their driver would come from the cell phone lot and pluck them up from the curb—assuming nothing interfered with the process.

Kirk closed the phone, praying madly. He'd have to find

the car the man had described, and then he'd have to decide whether he and the princess were going to get into the vehicle.

"What did you learn?"

"They'll have a car waiting for us." He shuffled forward as their line continued to move and prayed that they weren't headed into a trap.

Stasi took hold of Kirk's arm as he settled into the seat beside her. She felt blessed that they'd been able to secure a flight, and more blessed still to have boarded without seeing any more of Viktor's men.

But that didn't mean Viktor's men hadn't seen them. "Do you suppose Bosch will also have someone waiting for us at JFK?" Their flight was scheduled to last about two hours. Plenty of time for the men who were after her to assemble a welcome wagon.

"They seem to stay one step ahead of us wherever we go." Kirk's expression was resigned. "We'll just have to be quick on our feet. If we time it right with the Sanctuary car, we might be able to give them the slip. They shouldn't be able to try anything inside the airport—too much security. It's once we leave it that we'll be most vulnerable. In the meantime, try to catch some sleep. You couldn't have gotten much last night."

Stasi rested her head against his shoulder and sighed. She felt exhausted, not just physically, but emotionally drained from all the surprises that had been thrown at her. Her heavy eyelids closed.

Stasi kept tight hold of Kirk's hand as they zipped through the airport to meet the car that was coming for them. When he'd called to let them know they were ready, he'd asked the driver to phone him as he approached the curb. Stasi understood his motive. They needed to time it just right.

Whenever Kirk paused to look around, she took a moment to survey the crowd. Fortunately, she didn't recognize anyone. But that didn't mean no one recognized her.

"You don't suppose they've given up on finding us?" she asked.

"More likely they've realized we're on to them. They're staying out of sight—" He nearly jumped when his phone rang in his hand.

His conversation was short, and he tugged her toward the doors with a brief explanation. "They're almost to the curb. We need to be waiting."

A blue sedan approached.

"That's them." Kirk nodded, hesitating.

"Are we getting in?" Stasi felt his tension and uncertainty. They didn't know what they were getting into. She looked behind her at the glimmering reflections against the wide glass doors. Through the shifting images on the glass she caught sight of a figure standing still, one hand on his ear.

"I'm not sure—" Kirk began.

But Stasi hurried toward the car. "We don't have time to not be sure." She threw a nod in the direction of the man. "We're going."

She pulled Kirk after her, but as she slipped into the vehicle, the car began to pull away with Kirk still outside.

"Wait! What are you doing?"

# TWELVE

Stasi nearly climbed back out of the car, but the driver slowed, and Kirk dived in, pulling the door shut after them, just as the man who'd been trailing them stepped outside.

"Trying to leave without me?" He accused the driver, a grinning youth who appeared to be all of fifteen years old.

"I was. But if the princess wants you to come along, you can come."

"Can you get us out of here?"

"I'll try." The young man practically guffawed, and looked back at Stasi in the rearview mirror. "You're not Isabelle, are you?"

Stasi's heart hammered. "I'm Anastasia. Isabelle is my sister."

The driver laughed as he pulled into the flow of traffic. "I knew it—I knew it!"

Unsure what their driver's exclamations meant, Stasi exchanged worried looks with Kirk. They'd managed to escape the men at the airport, but what had they gotten themselves into?

The kid pulled into heavier traffic and talked as though he was doing nothing more strenuous than having tea. "They sent a team to find Isabelle. The whole place is buzzing, and then we get this phone call that the princess of Lydia is being held by some anonymous captor at JFK airport." He slapped the steering wheel. "I knew it had to be the other princess. Should I contact the cars behind us and tell them we don't need their backup?"

Confusing as his explanation might have been, Stasi's mind wrapped around one sentence in particular. "They sent a team to find my sister? I thought she was safe? She was testifying before the United Nations. My grandfather read all about it on the news."

"That was yesterday. Isabelle was supposed to go to a safe house today, but her car was hijacked."

"Hijacked!"

"They sent a team to pick her up."

"Is that going to work?"

"It should. Guess we'll find out."

"In the meantime—" Kirk cleared his throat "—don't call off the cars behind you. The man who was watching us got into that black sedan that's right behind us. Is he one of your men?"

"We're all in blue cars."

"Then please ask the drivers of the other cars to run some sort of interference. We can't let that car find out where we're going."

"I'm on it." Their driver simultaneously contacted the other drivers via his earpiece and weaved through traffic. Though he cut close to the other cars doing so, Stasi had to give him credit—he was moving them along quickly. If anyone was trying to follow them, they'd have their hands full.

While their driver strategized with the backup cars behind them, Kirk squeezed Stasi's hand, and she gave him a worried glance, only to be surprised by the expression on his face.

"What are you smiling about?"

"God is good."

"My sister's car was hijacked, and we're being driven through New York City by a twelve-year-old with Viktor Bosch's men on our tails."

"Nineteen," corrected their driver.

Stasi hadn't realized he was listening. "What's that?"

"I'm nineteen. But I get the twelve-year-old thing a lot."

Kirk chuckled from the seat beside her. His laugh was almost infectious enough to make her want to laugh, too, if she hadn't been so concerned about her sister. "Aren't you worried whether my sister is going to be okay or whether we're going to be okay?"

"It sounds like your sister is being rescued as we speak. I was worried whether we were going to be okay, but there was nothing to worry about." He gestured to their driver. "This guy could have been working for Bosch, for all we knew. That phone number could have led to anyone. As it is, we have backup." A blue sedan nearly cut them off, and their driver zipped around a corner at the same moment, leaving the black car that had been following them far behind.

"God was watching out for us." Kirk's eyes crinkled up at the corners as he settled back into his seat. "I suspect He's watching out for your sister, too."

"But her car was hijacked."

"True." Kirk offered her a slow smile. "Should we pray for her?"

Stasi nodded, and as they prayed, she felt her anxiety leave her. Was it possible Kirk could be right? Would God really see them through whatever was ahead, just as He'd seen them through so far? As they said amen, she looked back again, but couldn't see any further sign of the cars that had been following them. Had they finally lost them?

"Tell you what—" Kirk squeezed her hand "—let's go wherever this guy takes us, have a bite to eat, maybe catch a shower, and I suspect you'll see your sister again before nightfall."

The very thought of her sister sent tears springing to her eyes. "Do you think so?"

"Worrying won't get us there any faster."

Stasi wanted to point out that everything they'd learned so far had only hinted at a bigger, more complicated mess than they'd ever suspected when Kirk had first unblocked the door to her suite at the palace. But their prayer had revived her spirits, and she figured there was little point in protesting. She tried to do as Kirk instructed and stop worrying, but there were far too many uncertainties ahead.

In spite of his cracked rib, Kirk relaxed under the massaging showerhead, and let the clean water beat the stress and grime from him. Then he took the time to shave and dress in fresh clothes before going to look for Stasi.

From what they'd been told after arriving at the secret location in Manhattan, Kirk understood that Sanctuary International was a Christian asylum group that helped those who were trying to escape from persecution throughout the world. They'd had an agent on the ground, guarding Isabelle when the royal motorcade was ambushed, and Isabelle had been under the agent's protection until the hijacking earlier that day.

As a Sanctuary employee led him down the hallway of the vast, secret headquarters of Sanctuary International, Kirk heard a familiar laugh echoing through the hallway.

"Kirk!" Princess Anastasia looked radiant as she turned to greet him, her golden curls freed from their shroud and the grime of their five-day adventure washed away, replaced by the vibrant beauty who'd shunned him for the last six years. For a moment he held back, recognizing the distant woman instead of the friend he'd come to know.

But her smile was as friendly as any he'd seen the last few days, and more cheerful, too. She took his hand and pulled him toward the couple who rose from a sofa as he entered. He recognized Princess Isabelle immediately, as well as the man who'd been acting as her bodyguard prior to the ambush five days before.

"Isabelle was rescued," Stasi exclaimed, hugging the elder princess as Isabelle shook his hand. "And she's engaged. This is her fiancé, Levi Grenaldo. Levi's the agent who has been protecting her. His father, Nicolas Grenaldo, is the President of Sanctuary International. You wouldn't believe what they've been through."

As Kirk shook Levi's hand, the man explained, "We probably don't have time to tell the whole story again. We need to get to the bottom of what's happening in Lydia."

Kirk agreed. Though he was curious to know how the two of them had managed to escape the ambush unscathed, Levi was right. Lydia was in upheaval, and none of them would be safe until the whole mess was sorted out.

"And the best news," Stasi continued, "Isabelle says our brother Alexander survived the attack, as well."

Levi pulled out a picture. "This was taken in North Africa somewhere."

"There's been a great deal of upheaval in some of those parts of the world." Kirk looked at the grainy image.

"No more than we've been through. Of course, the man who told me Alexander is in North Africa is the same man who said you were in Milan." Isabelle crossed her arms and gave her sister a pointed look. "Which you're obviously not."

"But we were yesterday. It's reassuring to know Alec is alive, wherever he is. Whoever these people are after us, they haven't won."

"And we won't let them win," Kirk informed them with determination. "I know you two have been meeting with the

United Nations. Where do we stand? What is the situation in Lydia?"

Isabelle and Levi exchanged looks, and the elder princess spoke. "That's a long story—one we need to get caught up on ourselves. Can we get something to eat while we go over everything?"

Over the next couple of hours, Kirk learned more than he had ever wanted to know about international politics. He also learned that Stasi, in spite of her blond-haired, superficial image, was an insightful, intelligent, knowledgeable leader—not that he'd ever had any reason to doubt her, but her comments throughout their conversation only reinforced his respect for her.

The situation in Lydia was precarious. The Royal Crown and Parliament had always ruled in tandem with one another, providing a sort of checks-and-balances system as they sought to lead the small Christian nation. Now, with the monarchy in question and no royal ruler in place, the entire government found itself gridlocked in an impasse that wouldn't end until someone was crowned.

And as Kirk and Stasi had already learned, the members of the Royal House of Lydia were no longer the prime contenders for the throne. Though Basil of Lydia had run off to America to marry an actress shortly before the start of World War I, there was some question about whether he'd ever officially abdicated.

"Basil's father wasn't even king yet," Levi explained. "His grandfather was still on the throne. Valli insists that Basil never intended to give up the throne—that he would have returned to be crowned when the time came. But he died before that happened, and so his brother, Alexander the third, was crowned."

"But we have evidence that Valli has been conspiring against our family," Isabelle jumped in. "Which complicates the issue, because if Valli's claim to the throne was valid, why didn't he say something sooner? Why try to eliminate the royal family first?"

Stasi shook her head. "He's obviously covering up more than we know. I wonder what really happened with Basil? That was almost a hundred years ago."

"Valli is currently being charged with conspiracy," Isabelle assured them, "so he's currently out of the running for the crown, but there are a number of other parties involved. Valli himself claims to have been a pawn used by someone far more powerful than he is, but we don't know who that party is."

Stasi glanced at Kirk, who squeezed her hand. "That corresponds with what we've found. There's a conspiracy at work, and it goes back at least as far as Thad's disappearance six years ago. The Greek billionaires who were supposed to marry us were also involved."

"Yes." Isabelle nodded emphatically. "They most certainly were."

"I have Mother's journal," Stasi continued. "I read it—she wanted me to read it. She talks about the person who's behind all this. I don't think she knew his name. He went by a number." Stasi took a deep breath, and was surprised when her sister beat her to it.

"8."

"How did you know?" Kirk looked just as startled as she felt.

"I intercepted a week's worth of coded emails," Isabelle explained. "I'm still in the process of translating their contents, but whoever this 8 person is, he's been in cahoots with the Lydian military."

"General Lucca is holding our parents hostage in Milan."

"That's what I feared." Isabelle stood and crossed the room to where a Sanctuary staff member entered with a stack of papers. She dismissed the messenger with thanks and continued, "The two other generals, David Bardici and Marc Petrela, were also included on the emails in the conspiracy."

Levi rose to meet his fiancée as she slowly made her way back toward them, her eyes on the pages she'd been given. "What have you got?"

"The information we asked for on Stephanos Valli's brothers." She looked up, her face pale. "According to this family history, Basil of Lydia's daughter had two husbands and three sons. Her oldest son, Stephanos Valli, was the son of her first husband. They divorced, and some years later she relocated to Lydia and remarried, to the man who became the father to her next two children."

Stasi could tell her sister seemed to be having difficulty digesting what she read. "What can you tell us about her other two sons?"

Isabelle shook her head slowly. "Their names are David and Michael—" she swallowed "—Bardici."

Stasi jumped up and read over her sister's shoulder. "The same David Bardici involved in the email conspiracy? David Bardici, the Lydian general?"

"How many David Bardicis can there be?"

"David Bardici was appointed general four years ago." Kirk cleared his throat and stood, as well. "He'd been moving up quickly through the ranks after joining the military at a late age. I always wondered why he was promoted so quickly—I'd never found anything very impressive about him."

Clutching Kirk's hand, Stasi shook her head. "*Father* is the head of the military. He is the one who ultimately promoted Bardici to the rank of general. And he would have had a great deal of influence on Bardici's previous promotions, as well."

Isabelle balked visibly. "Why would Father promote someone who was out to get him? From what I've translated of these emails, Bardici was working with the conspirators who plotted to have our entire family killed."

"He sold his soul to the devil," Kirk murmured.

When Isabelle and Levi gave Kirk a strange look, Stasi explained, "It was something Thad said." She realized she hadn't even told her sister yet about what had really happened to their brother. "Thad ran away six years ago because of a deal Father made. He wouldn't be part of it, but he couldn't stop it, so he left."

Isabelle looked visibly relieved. "I always hoped you hadn't killed him," she told Kirk.

Kirk would have told Isabelle how much he appreciated her confidence in him, but his phone rang, and he glanced at the screen, then met Stasi's eyes. "It's your grandparents." He handed her the phone.

"Are you okay?" Stasi asked in place of hello. She listened for a moment, then happily shared with them the good news that Alexander, too, had escaped the attacks and had been spotted somewhere in northern Africa. When she thanked them again and closed the call, she updated everyone on what she'd learned.

"Gramma and Grampa were followed by three different cars. Grampa led them on a wild-goose chase, just like he promised, but he said eventually the men took off. They must have gotten word on our real whereabouts from the others who were after us."

Isabelle smiled. "I bet Grampa had a great time."

"I'm glad of that," Kirk agreed, "because it sounds like he provided enough distraction to help us get to New York. If those three cars had been after us, we likely never would have made it here."

Stasi's eyes widened. "It's staggering the kind of man-power they have after us. We've got to come up with a plan soon."

"I agree." Kirk nodded. "Let's outline our objectives."

"For one," Levi began, "we need to try to sort out the rest of who is behind these attacks, and how they all come together."

Stasi added, "The best place to do that is in Lydia."

"And, two—" Isabelle held up two fingers "—talk to Parliament. They can't do any official business until a ruler is crowned. It's been five days already, and they're starting to get antsy."

"The Lydian Parliament has been working with a United Nations peacekeeping team to find a solution that's acceptable to everyone," Levi explained. "It's only right that the Royal House of Lydia have a say in those conversations."

Stasi nodded. "Obviously that needs to be taken care of in Lydia, too. But there's a third thing. We need to get Dad back on his throne." She looked at Kirk with understanding. "You and I already took a crack at that and failed miserably."

Levi cleared his throat. "But we have the advantage of backup. Sanctuary International can bring a team in with us. We might have to take on Lucca and whoever is there guarding your father with him. But we'll do whatever we can to get King Philip back on his throne. In the meantime—" Levi looked at Kirk and Stasi "—we're going to have to split up. Isabelle and I can take a team to Milan. Do the two of you feel you can handle the situation in Lydia?"

"Do you have a backup team for us, too?"

Levi shook his head apologetically. "When Isabelle was hijacked, we discovered a breach in our security. Until we can be sure no one else is working as a double agent, we'll have to limit who we can trust. For the time being, I'm afraid we don't have any more agents to spare. You two will be safer working alone than you might be with a backup team."

"A backup team that would only stab you in the back," Isabelle added. "It's safest this way." Her expression turned imploring. "I hate to send you in without more support, but at the same time, we don't have the luxury of waiting. Kirk, surely you have friends in the royal guard—"

"Are you forgetting?" Stasi interrupted her sister. "Kirk is the most hated man in Lydia."

Kirk's hand rested on her shoulder. "I have a few friends I can trust. And they might be able to identify more. I can assemble my own team. There are still men in Lydia loyal to the crown. All we've got to do is pull them together."

"But, Kirk," Stasi protested, "it's going to be dangerous."

He leaned down and looked into her eyes. "You don't have to come. But I took a vow to protect the royal family. It's my duty."

Stasi swallowed. "You're injured. I have a duty to my people. *You're* the one who should be staying here, at least until you've had a chance to heal."

"Anyone might be on the throne by then." Kirk shook his head and turned resolutely to Levi and Isabelle. "I'm going."

"*I'm* going." Stasi all but stepped in front of him.

He looked down at her determined expression. He'd hoped she'd be willing to lie low and stay somewhere safe. Obviously, she wasn't that kind of princess.

# THIRTEEN

Kirk had no intention of letting anyone know Stasi was in Sardis unless he absolutely had to. In spite of Levi's warnings that Sanctuary International wouldn't be able to back them up, the organization was able to fly them back to Sardis in a private aircraft, avoiding possible detection from flying commercially. Kirk felt grateful for that.

Black clouds blocked the moonlight, helping to conceal them. Stasi kept her head down and her hair up under a hat, and Kirk's father rendezvoused with them at the underused landing strip outside the city in a car with dark-tinted windows. He took them straight to the Covingtons' cottage behind the castle.

"Why are there so many lights on in the palace?" Stasi peered out the window as they skirted the towering stone structure. "None of us are home."

Albert Covington cleared his throat and muttered something about usurpers.

His words were covered by Stasi's gasp. "My bedroom—there's someone in my bedroom! I saw a figure pass by the window." She reached forward from the backseat and patted Albert on the shoulder. "Please drive around again. I want to get a look at who was in my room."

"You'll need binoculars if you're going to recognize

anyone." Kirk hoped to get her to the relative safety of his parents' home before she was spotted.

"Do you have binoculars at your house?"

"We can probably find some for you."

"All right. Then let's go there."

"I'll warn you," Albert Covington cut in, "men from the palace guard came to the cottage yesterday and gave it a thorough search, looking for the two of you, accusing us of harboring fugitives." He blew out an impatient huff of air, as though the idea was absurd. "Theresa is still putting it back together, so don't mind the mess."

"Do you think the men will be back?" Kirk asked, alarmed by his father's revelation.

"I wouldn't think so, after they've just been here. Still, we should limit our comings and goings. If you can find somewhere else to lie low for a while, I'll take you there."

Once they reached the house, Kirk handed Stasi off to his mother before retreating to the small back room where he kept his things. His first objective was to get in touch with whoever might be on his side from the royal guard. Jason and Linus had come to his rescue at the pier, ultimately helping him get away from Viktor Bosch's men with nothing more than a cracked rib. And Galen had let them reach the helicopter on the guard station roof in exchange for a black eye.

Based on the sacrifices they'd made on his behalf, Kirk felt he could trust those three men. And perhaps they knew of more sympathizers to the throne. Jason and Linus had been intent on learning more about the attacks—perhaps they would have information to share. Kirk was determined to learn what he could, and waste no more time in doing so.

His father had picked up a TracFone and passed it along to him. The number couldn't be traced to them. It might not be a perfectly secure line, but Kirk only needed to reach them and arrange to meet—and he could accomplish that without any mention that might tip off a listener to where they were, or who was with him.

Three phone calls later, Kirk opened his door to find Stasi standing in the cottage hall, right hand raised as though to knock, a pair of binoculars in her left hand.

"There are too many trees to see the castle from here." She grabbed his hand. "We'll have to circle around the grounds."

Kirk wasn't convinced her plan was prudent. "Why is it so important that we find out who's in your room? It seems dangerous to leave the cottage unless we absolutely have to."

"Someone tried to have my family killed. Now there's a person in my room—and your mother has assured me that she left all the royal suites locked. No one has any right to be in there." Stasi looked at him imploringly. "This might be our chance to catch whoever's been breaking into my room— whoever barricaded me in there the day of the ambush."

"Can't we ask one of my parents to take a look?"

"From the glimpse I got when we passed by in the car, it looked as though they had opened my locked jewelry armoire. I need to see what they're messing with." Stasi pulled him down the hall toward the back door.

"So this is about jewelry?"

Stasi stopped short and spun around. Kirk nearly smashed into her, and got a very close-up look at the sparks that flashed in her eyes as she snapped at him. "I would think that our adventures over these past few days would have convinced you of the critical role jewelry can play in the rise and fall of empires. Somebody's after the—"

Holding up a hand to stop her before she could say the word *scepter*, Kirk realized how the words he'd spoken must have sounded. "I *am* convinced. I agree that whatever's going on with your jewelry is critical to sorting out the rest of what our enemies are after. But I'm also convinced that the intrigues surrounding those jewels is dangerous. We've nearly gotten captured or killed several times on account of all this jewelry. We need to err on the side of caution."

"Of course I plan to be cautious." Stasi's features softened. "That's why I bothered to bring you with me instead of going alone."

Her smart little smile sent his heart rate rocketing as they darted from the back door to the nearest trees, ducking into the woods that ran along the back wall of the castle. She lifted the binoculars to her eyes a few times, but seemed dissatisfied, and insisted on venturing farther for a better view.

With Stasi's attention focused on the castle windows, Kirk stayed alert to any difficulties on the ground. Queen Elaine had never allowed guard dogs on the same property as her children, but the royal guards had always roamed the perimeter of the royal estate. And Kirk had every reason to believe that Viktor Bosch, head of the royal guard, had only stepped up his security now that the royal family was gone—not to keep them safe, but to keep them out.

They reached a spot where the sloping ground rose higher, and Stasi finally seemed satisfied with the view. But her contented sigh quickly turned into a yelp of displeasure.

"Shh," Kirk placed a hand on her shoulder and tried to silence her. He hadn't seen any sign of trouble, but that didn't mean it wasn't close on their heels.

"It's a man. He has my jewelry armoire open." Stasi whispered harshly and cranked the dial on the binoculars. "If I can just get a clearer picture—"

"Let me try." Kirk pulled the binoculars from her hands and looked through them as he adjusted the picture. He cringed when he saw the figure inside. "Viktor Bosch!"

Stasi made a face. "That explains how he got into my locked room. The head of the royal guard has keys to everything. Do you think he's been searching for the scepter?"

"I don't know exactly where he fits into all this, but I'm

sure he's never liked me—at least not since your brother's disappearance."

"Do you suppose he's working for the generals?"

"Or he and the generals are working for 8."

A beam of headlights cut through the trees as Kirk spoke. He took Stasi's hand and pulled her back in the direction of his parents' cottage. "We've seen enough. Let's get moving."

He watched as the car pulled around to the back side of the palace, nearing his parents' cottage. Was someone on to them? After them?

The vehicle came to a stop, and so did Kirk, pulling Stasi close against him as he ducked behind a tree, peeking past the crook of a branch as the car doors opened and two large, masculine figures stepped out.

Stasi's hands gripped his shirt. "If we have to run, which way will we go?"

"I'm not sure." Kirk swallowed, his eyes trained on the shadows of the men's faces. The dark night didn't give him much to go on.

He trained the binoculars on the men just as the pair passed into the relative glow of a distant yard light.

"Linus and Jason." Kirk's shoulders sagged with relief. "They arrived much sooner than I expected them." Though he was glad to see them, at the same time, Kirk couldn't help but wonder what had fueled their urgency. Good news? No, good news could usually wait.

"Let's find out what they know. And pray it's good news." Stasi gave his hand a squeeze, and Kirk met her eyes. The same fear he felt was reflected there.

"Jason thinks we should meet somewhere else," Linus informed them as they ducked inside the cottage. "We've got more men on our side, but we can't risk meeting here, not right under everyone's nose."

"My family has a house in the country they rent out to tourists. It can accommodate twenty people overnight," Jason explained. "The folks who had it reserved for this week canceled their trip because of the ambush, so it's currently vacant. It's close to town, but on an underused lane with plenty of trees." He explained to Kirk how to find the spot.

"We'll leave in separate cars, ten minutes apart," Kirk decided. "Have the others meet us there. Is there room for my parents, as well?"

"Of course."

Half an hour later, eight of them sat around the large table at the country house, the curtains drawn, their heads bent low as they caught each other up on what they'd learned. Stasi helped Kirk's mother set out the impromptu meal of bread and cheese that Theresa had insisted on bringing along. The woman had also brought a cooler of food for breakfast—a reminder to Stasi of the talented woman's gifts for household management, that served her family in good times and bad.

"Viktor Bosch still has a price on your head, but only if you're brought in alive," Linus informed Kirk as he passed a heaping plate of artisan bread among them. "He's tripled the reward in the last three days."

When the guard quoted the purse, Kirk let out a low whistle. "The two of you could turn me in and retire comfortably far from here."

"And leave our country to chaos and ruin?" Jason scoffed. "I took a vow to protect the crown. So did you. As long as we're both working on the same side, I would no sooner betray you than I would Her Highness." He tipped his head to Stasi.

She returned a tense smile. "Your loyalty to my family will not go unnoticed—by the crown, or, I'm afraid, our enemies. I cannot guarantee our eventual victory. You may be rewarded for your efforts, or if the insurgents take control, you may be punished."

"That's a chance I'm willing to take," Jason assured her. "And there are many more in Lydia who feel the same way. We have not remained a Christian nation for nearly two millennia just to give it all away now."

"I hope you'll still feel that way when you learn how long our enemies' reach really is." Kirk began filling Jason and Linus in on what they'd learned—not only of Viktor's presence in Stasi's boudoir, but of the generals' conspiracy with the mysterious 8.

"According to what I've learned about this 8," Stasi explained, "he's made an agreement with my father for royal power. I don't understand the extent of it, but that's why my sister, Isabelle, got engaged to that awful Greek billionaire, and why Thad went into hiding." Stasi sorted out the facts as she spoke, and then blushed terribly, realizing she'd given away the fact that Thad was alive.

Both of the guards realized immediately what she'd done.

"So he *is* alive." Jason grinned.

"I never believed you killed him." Linus backed up his friend.

"He's only managed to stay alive because everyone thinks he's dead," Kirk reminded them, a steel-like glint in his eyes. "No word of his survival can leave this room. He must be kept secret and safe at all costs. If all else fails, he may be Lydia's last hope."

Linus nodded and stood. "All else has not yet failed. Though our resistance may be small, I'm convinced we have more sympathizers than have yet been willing to speak up." He sliced off another slab of cheese.

"I appreciate that," Kirk continued. "We'll need every man we can get before this is over, I'm afraid. Do you men know the latest on where Parliament stands?"

Jason passed his plate for more cheese. "The news coming from the Hall of Justice says Parliament is focused on reaching a compromise between the various contenders for the throne. The idea I've heard proposed is that all the descendants of Lydia who have any legal claim to the throne would rule together on some kind of board until the rightful ruler can be identified. That way, they're not crowning anyone who's not supposed to be crowned, but they're still following the law that insists the monarchy must be led by a descendent of Lydia."

"What's your source?" Linus challenged his friend. "The city is rife with rumors. I'd hate to act based on a half truth."

When Jason shrugged, Kirk's lips made a firm line, and he draped one arm over Stasi's shoulder. "We've got to have accurate information before we can do anything. We can't stick our heads up over some rumor."

"Like that rumor that there's something between you two?" Mischief sparkled in Jason's eyes. "I suppose there's nothing to that?"

Kirk pulled back his hands from around Stasi's shoulder, and felt all the more guilty when he saw the bright blush that colored her cheeks.

Linus laughed. "Thad was right all along, then. He always said he'd never give his little sister to any other man."

Jason chuckled, as well. "What was it he used to call you, Kirk?"

"Nothing," Kirk cut him off. "Nothing that's relevant right now. We've got a crown to restore and a country to save. Let's focus on that."

"We know what we know." Linus stood and stretched. "Jason and I will keep our ears to the ground for this 8 fellow. If Parliament makes a decision on the ruling council idea, we'll do whatever we can to back up Her Highness. In the meantime, we're off to round up more men."

Jason followed his friend to the door. "Chin up, Your Highness. You've got faithful servants in this nation yet."

The men ducked out in darkness and Kirk closed the door, locking it after them. When he turned back to the kitchen, he found his parents and the other men had left the room to settle into guest bedrooms, and Stasi cleared the rest of the dishes from the table by herself.

"I'm sorry if their jibes embarrassed you. I had no idea—"

Stasi looked up from setting plates in the sink, and tears twinkled in her eyes.

He reached for her instinctively, but she took a step back.

"Your Highness?"

"I've told myself a hundred times to leave you behind." Emotion reduced her voice to a whisper, and Kirk had to step closer just to be sure he heard her clearly.

She continued. "You're injured, Kirk. Bosch has got you associated with me. Still, I thought if I pretended there was nothing between us, then I could keep you from getting sucked down with me. But my pretending isn't fooling anyone, is it?"

Kirk's heart thumped so hard inside him he could hardly make out her strained words. "I'm not getting sucked down," he protested, torn between reaching for her again and letting her stand there uncomforted while she cried. "My injuries are not your fault."

She turned away as he reached for her, and he let his hand fall to his side again.

"You're a good man, Kirk Covington. A far better friend than I deserve. But this isn't your battle."

"It *is* my battle. I took a vow—"

"Please, keep your distance from me. For your own safety."

Kirk's stomach knotted. "No. You're tired. We're both jet-lagged. Get some sleep and we can discuss this in the morning."

Stasi nodded and took a few steps in the direction of her guest room. Before she reached the door to the small private suite, she looked back at him again. "What did Thad call you?"

For a moment, Kirk considered telling her, but realized that would likely only make the situation worse. He shook his head.

"Was it the same as your code name?"

"Yes."

"Why won't you tell me?"

"It doesn't change anything. It was a childish tease. There's nothing to be gained by sharing it."

With sad eyes, she gave him a long look before ducking into the room and closing the door after her.

Kirk headed to his room at the other end of the guest house, past his parents' bedroom door, where a dim light shone from under the crack of the door, indicating they were still awake and likely rehashing the evening's discussion.

Exhausted, Kirk left them to their conversation, and set about getting ready for bed with a heavy heart. He needed his sleep. The situation in Lydia had been building, and he felt as though it was gearing up for a showdown. Anything could happen the next day, and most likely would.

And in spite of her push to keep him away, Kirk had no intention of letting Stasi face it alone.

# FOURTEEN

Jason's country guest house swarmed with activity when Stasi emerged from her suite the next morning. A cluster of men in soldier's uniforms had their heads bent over the coffee table, the television blaring a newscast just beyond them.

Linus and Jason had returned with backup and occupied the table with open laptops and a scattering of papers. Stasi also recognized Galen, his black eye already mellowed to a dull yellow-green.

Glad as she was that she'd taken the time to shower and dress in her en suite bathroom before emerging, Stasi couldn't help wondering what she'd missed.

"What's this floor plan belong to?" She looked over the shoulders of the men to the blueprints that occupied the center of the table.

"The Hall of Justice," Kirk answered from near the coffee pot. "Parliament has issued a call for all those with a claim to the throne to sign an agreement to rule together by consensus until the rightful ruler can be found." He held out a fresh mug to her. "Coffee?"

Stasi let out a long breath. "Coffee would be great. What are the terms? I'm not signing anything I haven't thoroughly read."

"It's sixteen pages." Kirk handed her a sheaf of papers and

the steaming mug. "Would you like cream or sugar?" His eyes met hers over the mug, and Stasi saw lingering sadness there.

She paused, for a moment forgetting whatever they'd been discussing as his fingers brushed hers in the passing of the cup. Part of her wanted to take back what she'd said the night before. But another louder part shouted for her to make him sign an agreement to stay far away from the danger that followed her everywhere.

"No cream or sugar," she said finally. "It's not a cream or sugar sort of day, is it?"

As he stepped back, Kirk gave her a wink.

Stasi felt her stomach dovetail. "And what about the soldiers in the living room?"

"Isabelle gave us a name—Sergio Cana. The others are his trusted allies."

Stasi nodded, remembering. The soldier was a friend of her brother Alexander, and had helped Isabelle and Levi more than once in the past week. "But what are they doing here?"

"You've got to sign the agreement in person." Kirk's expression was somber. "Linus heard rumors that Bosch intends to keep a close eye on the Hall of Justice. If you show up there—"

"But Bosch and his men wouldn't dare make a move in such a public place. They could be charged with treason."

"They could. But only if their mission fails. If they remove your family from the picture, there won't be anyone to charge them with treason." He looked at the soldiers and back to her, and his lips pinched together with displeasure. "You won't go alone."

It took Stasi a moment to connect all the dots. She pictured herself walking into the Hall of Justice with Kirk at her side, but realized that was foolish. No doubt just getting inside the

Hall of Justice would be tricky. Besides, she'd told Kirk to keep his distance.

The man knew how to follow orders.

Settling into the nearest unoccupied chair, Stasi turned her attention to the documents in front of her. Sixteen pages was a lot to read, especially when she could hardly make it through the first sentence without thinking about Kirk.

There were still too many variables outside of their control, and Kirk felt the lapse acutely. The Hall of Justice was too large a building, for one thing, with far more entrances and exits than they could cover. And he wasn't about to rely on the existing security—if there were security personnel on hand at all, he suspected they might be working for anyone. No, it wouldn't do to trust them.

Then, of course, there was the issue of transportation. With the bulletproof royal limousines destroyed in the ambush on the motorcade the week before, there was nothing in the royal garage that would protect the princess. Besides that, he wasn't convinced they should try to get anything out of the garages, since it would mean going back to the palace, and he knew he'd overstepped his welcome there as far as Viktor Bosch was concerned. They'd have to use their own cars, but none of them were bulletproof.

He seriously considered putting Stasi in body armor.

Ultimately he knew it came down to the fact that he didn't like letting her out of his sight—not with all the threats against her. But she'd asked him to stand down. He had to respect her decision, even if he didn't agree with it.

Stasi answered her phone and waved him over. Kirk stood by her chair until she closed the call, then crouched down in the crowded room so he could talk to her.

"Isabelle and Levi are planning to meet with Father this morning. They heard the news about the ruling council and are hoping to fly into Sardis by noon. They don't want to come without Mother and Father, but you and I both know they'll have their hands full prying them away from Lucca and his men." She reached for his hand and gave it a squeeze.

Her gesture gave him hope, as did her words. "If your father could be convinced to return, perhaps you won't have to sign anything. Should we wait?"

For a long moment she looked him full in the face, her small hand kneading his fingers worriedly. Finally, she stood and pulled him toward the relative privacy of the kitchen. Ducking into the small space between the refrigerator and the corner cupboards, she whispered, "Mother's journal raised issues about the agreements Father made with 8 and some of his associates. If the deals he made came to light, he wouldn't be eligible to rule. He could be charged with treason."

"I wonder, then, why Valli and the generals haven't exposed him. You'd think they'd use what they have to get the king off his throne."

"As long as Father is willing to work with them, they've nothing to gain by exposing the deals they've made with him. They must still feel he's more useful to them, perhaps as a means of leading them to the scepter. Besides, there's a good chance in exposing him, they'd divulge their own hand in all of it. They can't risk that."

"I suppose you're right. If your father came back to claim the throne and turned his back on their deal, they'd no doubt set up someone to take the fall on their behalf." Kirk hadn't realized when he'd stepped into the nook by the cupboards just how small the space was.

Stasi's earnest face looked up at him from mere inches away, and the light scent of vanilla undertones from her coffee only made her that much more appealing. "What do you think I should do?"

"I think…" Kirk began slowly, trying to generate a thought

beyond the image of her closer in his arms, but there was little use to that.

Her hands traced a line down his cheek. "Your injuries are healing," she noted softly. Her touch felt so gentle, so irresistibly sweet.

"Let me accompany you to the Hall of Justice," he implored quietly.

"So you think I should go, even if my father may be on his way?"

Kirk tried to straighten out just what it was he thought. Mostly he wanted to be somewhere a bit more private with her than the kitchen, with a lot less to worry about than the future of Lydia. "Your father's arrival won't change the Bardici's claim to the throne. Ultimately, both you and your sister need to sign the covenant, but it's going to be dangerous, whatever you choose." He brushed back a lock of her blond hair, which was still damp from her shower. "I want to be with you."

"I'd never forgive myself if anything happened to you." Stasi had somehow gotten taller, or perhaps risen up on her tiptoes. The tip of her nose brushed his.

"Kirk!"

Kirk jumped backward at the gruff sound of his father's voice.

"I need to speak with you. Outside."

The grim set of Albert Covington's jowls made Kirk feel as though he was a little boy again, caught in some dreadful mischief. In fact, the only time he could recall his father looking quite so angry was on the fated day when he was twelve years old and had been told to stay away from Anastasia.

He excused himself from Stasi and followed his red-faced father out to the garage.

"She's a princess!" Albert hadn't quite gotten the door shut after them before he started in. "More than that, she's the only hope this country has right now, and I won't have you seducing her."

"I wasn't—" Kirk began, feeling all the more like the boy who'd been scolded half his lifetime ago.

"Son, I've tried to tell you. I've asked you. I've begged you. You can run after any other girl in the kingdom, but leave the princess alone."

With all that was hanging over them that day, Kirk couldn't stand that his father would press the issue. Rather than take his father's words as law as he always had before, Kirk countered, "This isn't about me and Stasi, is it, Dad? There was only one girl in all of Covington you weren't supposed to go near. Mom got sent off to Europe, but it didn't change the way you felt about her."

His father's red face became, if possible, that much redder. "Leaving Georgia tore our families apart. It took them ten years before they would speak to either of us, and fifteen years to speak to each other. The greatest mistake of my life was running off to Lydia with your mother."

"Why?" Kirk didn't understand. "You love her, don't you?"

"Of course I do. It's because I love her that I can't stand what we did to our families. You hardly knew your grandparents. I wanted to go home last week when the ambush first struck, but as your mother said, where would we go? We can't go home now. This is the only home we have left, and I won't have you tearing it apart by disgracing Her Royal Highness." He took a breath, and a little of the furious red drained from his face. "Have you seen the way she looks at you?"

"I can't help how she—"

"Yes, you can. You've been leading her on all this time. It's not fair to her."

"I'm not leading her on. If anything, I've been trying to push her away."

"Not from what I've seen. You love her. Deny it!"

"I can't deny it."

His father headed for the door. "You've got to deny it—for her sake and the sake of Lydia. Our country is caught up in a vicious tug-of-war, and we need every man we can get pulling on our side."

"I'm trying."

"No, you're not. You're distracting the princess." With that, Albert left the garage and pulled the door shut after him.

Kirk scowled. Much as he'd tried to deny—to himself and everyone else—his feelings for Stasi, his father had hit the nail on the head. He did love Stasi. But his father was also correct when he said that he had no right to her.

And if the unfolding plans were any indication, Stasi had a future in politics ahead of her. The nation of Lydia needed her leadership. She didn't need him as a distraction.

He pulled his phone from his pocket and looked at the screen, debating. Dialing his grandfather in Georgia, Kirk kept the conversation brief. "If my parents return to Georgia, can they stay with you?"

His grandfather let out a long, low chuckle. "You know, I've been wondering for years what it would take to bring them back home. Apparently, from what I see on the news, it takes a country torn apart."

"So you're not still so angry with them for running away together that you won't even speak to them?"

"Son, I got over that years ago."

Kirk closed his eyes, his heart pounding. "Maybe you should tell them that."

"Maybe I should." His grandfather sounded thoughtful. "Maybe this insurgent uprising wasn't all a bad thing. You wouldn't want to come home, too, would you? The local sheriff is always looking for deputies. They'd love to have someone with your background."

"I don't know." Kirk wasn't even sure what a deputy did.

He thought about the Westerns he'd loved as a kid. It was a different world over there in America. But moving to the United States would give him an excuse to leave Stasi. If he couldn't be around her without acting on the growing feelings between them, then for her sake, he needed to leave.

"Maybe that's something I could look into. I need to go." He closed the call with his grandfather and then looked at his phone.

Sure, he enjoyed Georgia, but could he leave Lydia and Stasi behind?

Did he have any other choice?

Stasi grabbed Kirk's hand as he came back inside and pulled him toward the television. "Breaking news report," she explained.

"What has Parliament decided now?"

"Not them—the weather. There's quite a squall moving across the Mediterranean. It's expected to hit Lydia in two hours. Isabelle's plane may not be able to land. They might not even take off." She watched his face as he absorbed the news. "What do you think we should do?"

Kirk looked thoughtful. "We've been praying all along that God would help us, haven't we?"

"Yes."

"Do you suppose this is His way of helping?"

"By sending a storm?" Linus asked from near his elbow, where he watched the radar image of the swirling storm clouds.

"Do you know anyone else who controls the weather?" Kirk challenged.

Stasi couldn't help but smile at the image Kirk's words evoked, of God riding up on a storm cloud to save them just like in the Bible stories of old. The kings and queens of Lydia had changed many times since Acts chapter sixteen first mentioned its founder, but God hadn't changed. And God was ultimately the leader of their small nation. "Should we try to time our visit to Parliament to correspond with the storm?"

"What do you think?" Kirk looked around the room at the men who'd assembled.

"There will likely be some confusion the moment the storm hits," Galen noted. "If we arrive just before the storm, we could take advantage of that window of time when our enemies will be most distracted. It may not be much of an advantage."

"If it's the only advantage we have, we should use it." Jason looked convinced.

"I agree." Stasi took a deep breath. They were going to go through with it, then. "That means we should leave in an hour and a half. Can we be ready by then?"

"We can."

"We will."

"We don't have much choice."

The men all seemed to agree, so Stasi encouraged them to make their final preparations. As they bent over their maps, Kirk leaned close to her.

"Where do you want me?"

Stasi couldn't help looking into his eyes, and her breath caught. She could think of a lot of places she wanted him to be—mostly as far from danger as possible. And she wished she could go with him.

"You can't go in, Kirk. You're injured. It's too much of a risk."

"We don't have enough men to cover the whole building. You need everyone you can get."

"There's something to be said for that." She tried to think. Every time she tried to envision herself walking into the Hall of Justice, her stomach knotted with the same sickening fear that had left her retching over the side of Kirk's sailboat a week before. Having him nearby would have a comforting effect on her nerves. She already knew that from much practice.

"You can ride with me. But when we reach the front doors, fall back. A team will accompany me inside. You'll stay posted at the front doors."

For a long moment, Kirk's expression remained too stony to read. But then his lips bent up with a resigned smile.

"If anything seems amiss, don't hesitate to come right back out," Kirk cautioned Stasi as the car rumbled along the cobbled streets to the Hall of Justice. "We can always try again another time. If anything happens to you, there won't be another time."

Stasi simply squeezed his hand, her eyes trained on the dark clouds that rolled ever nearer. The wind, which had been eerily still for most of the last hour, had begun to pick up, whipping flags and tree branches with sudden gusts. The streets were likewise unusually empty—whether because of the pending storm or the political turmoil, Kirk wasn't sure, but it gave him an odd sense of foreboding.

Kirk returned the squeeze, wishing Stasi didn't have to go through what was about to happen, or at the very least, that he could guarantee she'd come through it just fine. But neither of those options was on the table. "If at any point you feel you're in over your head, we can turn around. You don't have to go right now."

"Now is as good a time as any, and probably the best shot we'll get. We can't leave the country to the Bardicis to hand over to 8. This is the only way I can stop them."

The first fat drops of rain began to spatter down as Kirk led Stasi from the car to the doors of the Hall of Justice. The other two cars that accompanied them came to a stop, and their men filed out. As promised, Kirk waited just under the porte cochere while Stasi continued inside with two men in front of her, and two behind.

The security guards standing just inside the door wore sunglasses, in spite of the rain. Kirk tried to get a decent look at them before the doors went shut, but didn't see enough of either man to determine if they were friend or foe. He certainly wasn't going to trust them to stop anyone who might head in after Stasi.

They hadn't advertised the time of their arrival. He hoped Stasi could get her signature on the documents and be back out before anyone realized she was even in Sardis.

Kirk reached inside his pocket and felt for the push-to-talk switch that connected to the microphone attachment of his earpiece security kit. Galen and his men had driven halfway around the building to the side doors. Another man, Simon, took his position on the other side of the porte cochere from Kirk.

Across the street, Kirk caught sight of his father fiddling with his earpiece. Albert Covington was connected by phone to Theresa, who'd taken a van to the rural landing strip in hopes that Isabelle's plane would be able to land. They'd had no contact with the elder princess all that morning, and could only pray her contingent had made their flight. No doubt she and Levi had their hands too full to call. He could only pray it was because they were en route to Sardis.

For several long, anxious minutes, nothing seemed to be happening. Kirk had almost begun to hope they'd make it through the signing without incident when he saw his father answer his phone across the street. Albert's face blanched, and a moment later he darted over, one hand on the driver's door of the car Kirk and Stasi had arrived in, which was still parked with the other two vehicles, awaiting their departure.

"Isabelle landed. Your mother picked them up," he shouted

across to Kirk, not bothering with his earpiece. "They're being followed by five cars."

"Go!" Kirk yelled, waving him off.

Albert got inside the car and pulled away. The private landing strip wasn't far outside the city. He'd have little trouble finding Theresa—but what was one car against five?

Kirk squeezed the transmitting button and spoke into his microphone. "We've got tails on Princess Isabelle's car. Five vehicles." He paused for just a second. Much as he hated pulling men away from Stasi's security detail, they'd lose everything if Isabelle was caught—especially if she had her father with her. And if the men didn't hurry, they might not catch up to Albert. "Galen, can you spare a car?"

"No problem. We're half-asleep over here. I'm sending a driver out now."

Simon leaped out from under the porte cochere to the rear vehicle. "Will you be all right if I leave?"

Kirk hesitated. Should he send the man? His mother was outnumbered and in need of assistance. Surely Stasi was safe at the Hall of Justice. They had little more to fear than the storm that threatened to unleash its rage around them.

The transmitting device at his ear relayed his father's voice, "Backup—" The transmission cut out, but the fear in his father's voice had carried through clearly. "I need backup—now!"

He looked to the soldier across from him. "Go. Head for the landing strip outside of town. I'll keep Stasi safe. Come back for us as if you can."

The man nodded and leaped into the driver's seat, peeling out and away.

Kirk went back to his station, his heart hammering out a prayer for his mother's safety. And his father's. And Isabelle's. And Stasi's.

They were down to one car in front, and one in back with

Galen. It would be enough. It had to be enough. Surely Stasi would exit any moment, and they could safely make their getaway.

He stood back and prayed. Even the storm seemed to hold its breath. Tense. Waiting.

Long minutes crawled by, and Kirk itched to know what was keeping Stasi. Had some long-winded bureaucrat insisted on reading the whole sixteen-page covenant? Or was Stasi in trouble?

A gust of wind and rain hit with fury.

From up the street Kirk heard a squeal of tires. He trotted a few steps away from the building—just enough to give him a decent glimpse of the cross streets ahead.

His mother's van swept by, followed quickly by two vehicles he didn't recognize. Then came his father, swerving crazily between two lanes. Kirk felt glad that the storm had kept people off the streets. None of the cars appeared to be traveling at a safe speed.

But they were making their way closer to the Hall of Justice.

The transmitter at his ear buzzed to life again. "Stasi has signed the document," Sergio informed them in a quiet tone. "She's embracing Prime Minister Emini, and then we'll be making our way out through the front of the building."

Kirk watched as two more cars swept past. Would Isabelle be able to stop and sign the covenant?

"I hate to bust up your party," Galen's transmission cut in from his post at the back door. "Some men just got past me. They knocked me out for a minute there. Sergio, they're probably headed your way."

Gripping his transmitting button, Kirk debated how to respond. There was no answer from Sergio—no doubt he and his men were too busy dealing with the situation to stop and give them an update. Though his boots itched to run inside and tackle the men who'd come in, if he left his post at the door, anyone might get in after him. And the cars that had gone screaming past earlier were rumbling up the hill again.

His mother's van tore up the street toward him, her determined face just visible through the windshield. He suspected she was going to try to let off the princess at the door. There was just room enough for her van to get by next to the other waiting car, but a red coupe was tight on her tail. As the street widened, branching off to the front drive that dipped past the porte cochere where Kirk stood, the coupe pulled alongside his mother's vehicle, forcing her away from the Hall of Justice.

She swept past, taking the next corner at a quick clip. Kirk had little doubt she'd come back around for another try if she could. Though he hadn't been able to make out much through the darkened back windows of the van, it appeared she had several people inside. Had Isabelle managed to convince the king to return? Kirk wasn't about to distract anyone by asking.

In the meantime, his mother's entourage swept past him, save for one car that swerved toward him. It didn't belong to their group. In fact, it looked as though the driver intended to take a swipe at him.

With a tall marble pillar blocking him in on one side, Kirk leaped backward into a bush just as the car all but clipped his ankles.

The car screeched to a halt and three figures hurried out, darting into the building, right past the guard, who did nothing to stop them. If anything, they waved them on.

Kirk untangled himself from the bush just as the car drove off. But there was no mistaking who'd gone inside the Hall of Justice. Kirk would recognize his boss anywhere.

Viktor Bosch. He and his men had their guns drawn.

# FIFTEEN

Kirk no longer felt he had any choice. He'd failed to keep Bosch and his men from entering, but he couldn't let them reach Stasi. He ran into the building after them, and heard the guards stationed at the doors shout as he darted past.

At any second, he expected them to tackle him from behind, but the only sound he heard was the wet soles of his boots squeaking as he tore down the wide marble halls.

The Chamber of Parliamentary Session lay behind two heavy wood doors. As Kirk raced toward them, he saw Viktor pull the door open, and he and his men stepped inside.

Skidding toward the entrance in his wet boots, Kirk opened one door in time to reveal chaos inside the room.

Prime Minister Gloria Emini was being shuffled off through a back exit. Sergio and his men fought the insurgents who'd breached Galen's guard, and it took Kirk a moment to spot Stasi, shoved back behind the large oak lectern on the dais.

Viktor must have spotted her at the same moment, because he rushed forward down the carpeted aisle. Vaulting the back rail, Kirk bounded across the semicircular rows of seats toward the front. He leaped to the dais just as Viktor approached it.

Throwing himself over Stasi, he tried to hide her behind the cover of the podium.

"Kirk!" Stasi clung to his shirt.

A shot rang out, and Stasi flinched in his arms. Kirk expected at any moment to feel a sting of pain. "Are you hit?" He tightened his hold on her.

"I'm fine. We need to get out of here."

Kirk risked looking out past the podium. Linus had apparently disarmed Viktor Bosch and had engaged him in hand-to-hand combat.

"Where are the other men who came in with Viktor?"

He doubted the other men would have turned tail and run, but he could see no sign of them. Glancing up the side aisle, he saw a clear path to the double doors he'd entered through. If they could make it out of the room, hopefully they could escape the building. Both he and Stasi wore body armor under their clothing, but the only vest he'd been able to find in Stasi's small size wasn't rated for high-impact weaponry, and it left most of her shoulders uncovered.

He'd have to shield her as much as possible.

"Ready?"

She nodded.

"Toward the double doors. Let's go." They scrambled forward and leaped off the raised dais.

At that moment, Viktor Bosch landed a blow on Linus's jaw that sent him spinning back. The guard landed with a thump on the floor.

Kirk froze. There wasn't time to get Stasi back behind the raised podium again.

Bosch lunged toward a gun that lay a few meters away, up the aisle. Though it left the princess unshielded for a moment, Kirk vaulted after the man, landing solidly on his back and sending him sprawling.

Stasi's small feet darted past his line of sight, headed toward the gun.

There was no time to see if she was able to pick it up. Bosch rolled sideways, and Kirk jumped backward, getting to his feet just in time to grab Viktor by the back of his shirt, throwing him away from the direction in which he'd seen Stasi run.

The man aimed a fist at Kirk's ribs, apparently aware of his weak point, but Kirk ducked. He caught a glimpse of Stasi hunkered down between two rows of seats, and thought about encouraging her to make a run for it. But he knew the guards at the front doors sided with Viktor, and he doubted they'd let her pass. No, Stasi would be better off sticking close to him for now.

Kirk tried to kick out, to knock Bosch's legs out from under him, but the aisle was too narrow to permit free movement. Instead, he barreled into the man, pushing him down the inclined floor toward the center of the room.

The man grunted and lunged back.

Jumping to the side, Kirk got out of Viktor's way just enough for his attacker to go sprawling forward. Kirk sprung over him and scooped up Stasi from her aisle. "Let's go."

She ducked under his arm and they headed for the door. Kirk kept her slightly ahead of him, aware that Viktor could come up behind him at any moment. Seconds later he felt a hard jerk on his ankle, and his leg was yanked out from under him, sending him down.

He rolled onto his back and got his knees up just as Viktor flew feet-first toward his chest. Catching him instead with the soles of his boots, Kirk pushed the man backward down the aisle and scrambled back to his feet. He lurched forward, his arm once again held high over Stasi, offering her what little cover he could, when the doors ahead of them burst open.

Men poured in. At first Kirk wasn't sure whose side the

strangers were on, but then he recognized Levi with Isabelle under his arm.

"The covenant is on the podium!" Stasi shouted at her sister.

Isabelle ran for the central dais.

Kirk had half a mind to caution them against coming in, but they had brought enough manpower with them to tip the odds back in their favor. As Viktor Bosch lunged toward him again, one of Levi's men stepped between them, landing a solid punch on Viktor's jaw.

"Get moving," the agent shouted back at Kirk, as Isabelle and Levi scurried down the aisle toward the covenant that needed Isabelle's signature.

Spotting Stasi still mostly hidden in one of the semicircular rows of seats, Kirk scrambled to her side and pulled her to her feet. "Let's go," he whispered, but had barely spun around when the men who'd arrived with Viktor ducked out from behind a pillar, their guns pointed solidly at Stasi.

Kirk had only a second to pull the princess behind him before the guns went off. Bullets clipped the chairs next to him, and he felt another slam into his body armor, knocking his breath from his lungs.

Gulping air, Kirk caught a glimpse of a man bounding through the heavy wood doors at the pair of gunmen.

The distraction gave him just the break he needed. Kirk pulled Stasi after him, but her scream a second later stopped him short. Before he could ask if she'd been hit, she cried out.

"Father?" Stasi stumbled toward King Philip, who'd knocked one gunman cold and slammed the other's fingers against the marble pillar until the gun fell from his hands.

"Run!" King Philip shouted. "Get Stasi out of here."

Kirk hesitated. He couldn't leave the king behind. He was a sentinel with the royal guard. He'd taken a vow to protect the crown.

"No!" Viktor Bosch shouted, advancing toward them.

"Run!" King Philip cried again, his eyes boring into Kirk's. "Keep Stasi safe!"

Unable to argue with the king's royal command, Kirk pulled Stasi under his arm and retreated toward the door. They burst into the marble hallway just as a shot rang out.

Kirk sprinted forward with Stasi at his side, surprised to see the guards had left their post at the door after all. He and Stasi spilled out under the porte cochere to find a world whipped by rain and wind. The waiting car was gone, and with sinking dread Kirk realized the crafty guards had likely stolen their getaway vehicle. Nor did he see any sign of his mother or her car. Nothing but dark clouds and howling wind waited outside.

"Now what?" Stasi asked him breathlessly.

With a quick glance back through the closing front door, Kirk spotted Viktor headed down the hallway toward the front doors.

"Run!" Kirk gripped Stasi's hand and tore off down the street, adjusting his pace so Stasi could keep up with him. He ran around the side of the building, hoping Galen and his men still had their last car, but there was no sign of anyone, man or vehicle. Doubling back, he pulled Stasi along after him.

"Where are we going?"

Where was there to go? The Hall of Justice sat on a bluff overlooking the marina. Rather than try to climb higher up the hill, Kirk turned toward the water. "To the boats. Maybe we can lose them there." He hoped his mother, or one of their other drivers, would come along with a car any moment, but there was no sign of any traffic activity in the midst of the howling storm.

Already the rain had soaked them almost to the skin. Kirk glanced back and caught sight of Viktor running after them.

From what he could tell of the drill-sergeant officer, the man was in excellent shape. And it was less than a block to the marina.

He couldn't let him catch up to the princess.

"The pier!" Kirk scanned the marina. Where were the Jet Skis that belonged to the Royal Guard? Would his fingerprint still work to free them from their security moorings? There was nowhere else to turn, and he wasn't about to try to swim for it. That option hadn't worked out very well for him before.

With no alternative, Kirk pulled Stasi down the dock, the hollow echoes of their pounding feet lost amid the screams of the storm.

"Where?" Stasi panted as they neared the end of the pier.

"Jet Ski. Get on."

He settled onto the craft behind her and reached up to the box whose electronic sensor was shielded from the elements by a thick waterproof barrier of clear vinyl. Kirk mashed his thumb against the surface and waited, glancing back to see Viktor barreling down the dock toward them.

Green.

He flipped open the security box, tugged the mooring free and pulled the Jet Ski key from its hook. Jamming it in the ignition, he got the engine powered up just as a shot went off behind him, sending water spraying up beside them. Much as he'd have liked to steal the key for the other craft, there wasn't time to mess with another security box. Not without Bosch catching up to them.

"Stay low," Kirk cautioned Stasi, trying to cover her as much as he possibly could as he steered them away from the pier. Another shot slammed into the back plate of his body armor, but already the agile craft had begun mounting the swelling waves, putting some space between him and the dock, and the shot didn't hit him as hard as the first one had.

For a few moments, his battle was only with the sea.

Frothing, churning waves beat against the pier, threatening to crush their small craft against the pilings. Kirk focused on keeping the Jet Ski pointed at an angle to the waves, riding between the swells, making headway toward the islands.

In another moment he heard the drone of a motor, and looked back to see Viktor steering after them.

Kirk coaxed the watercraft forward. As they sped away from shore, he found the storm was mostly drenching rain, with winds limited to agitated gusts. Though the soggy sky had long ago soaked them both, and Kirk felt the onerous weight of his body armor, as long as they were able to avoid swamping waves, he hoped to increase the distance between their craft and Viktor's. The islands offered the possibility of cover, and even some potential for losing Bosch among the many inlets and coves.

He sped toward the nearest island, picking up speed in the open water. The jagged waves slapped and jarred the craft, and Kirk kept a tight hold on Stasi as he covered her hands to steer. The occasional large wave drenched them both, reminding Kirk of the risk they'd taken heading out to sea in body armor. If either of them slipped from the Jet Ski, the weight of their vests would pull them down quickly.

He couldn't let that happen.

With the advantage of his knowledge of the islands to guide him, Kirk swerved past the first, small island, which was little more than a long spit of sand. Its domed stretches of white beaches were a magnet for tourists, but repellant to him. They needed cover. The bare sand offered little of that.

But it did give him a blockade to put between him and Bosch, who chugged relentlessly after them in spite of the drenching rain. Swerving wide past the sand spit, Kirk turned to their watercraft toward the next island, a rocky, beach-rimmed promontory whose palm trees waved and shook in the storm.

There was an inlet on the back side of the island, which led to a lagoon at the center of the atoll. Kirk headed toward it, hoping to duck inside, but aware that the fortress could become a prison if Viktor followed them in. Once they entered the lagoon, there would be no way back to the sea except via the narrow inlet, allowing them only one possible route of escape via watercraft.

Kirk pointed the watercraft toward the narrow inlet, his mind racing.

Stasi craned her head around and shouted against the whipping wind. "No! There's no way out once we're in—and nowhere to hide inland."

She was right. The sparse palm trees wouldn't conceal them for long.

The Sardis archipelago offered dozens of islands, and many more options of places to hide. Though he was eager to get Stasi out of the drenching rain, at the same time, he had the right to be picky about where they hid. Viktor hadn't backed off their tail, but neither had he gained on them.

They still had time.

Kirk swerved through several more islands, dismissing most without any deliberation. Many were simply too flat, too sparse, too small to offer them anywhere to hide.

He swerved past another stretch of islets and spotted a long wall of rock.

"Channel Island!" Stasi called back to him. "We can hide there!"

Kirk nodded and headed them in that direction, but he knew the ominous thudding of his heartbeat wasn't just from the pursuer who continued to dog their tail.

Channel Island was a lengthy, washed out atoll—two curving strips of land with a stretch of water between them. But the water that flowed between them was no shallow bath. Born from a long-dead volcano, the water below was deep and dark, rimmed with jagged rocks, and given to fierce undertows. Especially during storms.

Their Jet Ski chugged as it cut through the slapping waves. The menacing rock walls of the island's twin promontories guarded the channel on either side, imposing and foreboding.

It was too risky.

"No." Kirk turned their craft away from the island.

Stasi fought him for control of the handlebars. "We have to take cover. I'm tired and cold. I don't know how much longer I can hold on."

It was true, her lips had taken on a bluish tint. But they'd take on a far deeper blue if the vicious undertow caught them. "It's not safe." Kirk used his greater strength to pull the watercraft wide of the island. "There are too many hidden rocks, and the undertow is deadly."

Stasi sagged on the seat in front of him, whether from defeat or exhaustion, Kirk wasn't sure.

"We'll find a hiding place." He pointed the craft toward the next less-than-promising island. "I'll keep you safe." Though the oath came from his heart, in his head, he wondered how he could possibly accomplish it. They were running out of islands. Already the protected cove of the keys was giving way to the force of the storm on the wide-open sea.

Their trip was becoming more dangerous. And, he realized as he glanced behind them, Viktor was gaining on them.

All their swerving about had cost them precious time. Determined to lose their pursuer, Kirk gunned the Jet Ski to greater speeds. He thought about trying to circle back to Sardis, but looping back around would essentially take them through Viktor's path. It would only bring them closer to danger, not farther from it. And it would waste precious fuel.

As Kirk recalled, the Jet Skis could only make an eighty- or ninety-kilometer trip in perfect weather. Given the rough seas, their fuel efficiency would be much less. And the

Sardis archipelago stretched nearly fifty kilometers from the mainland.

With a sinking stomach, he realized they might have already passed the point of no return. They likely no longer had enough fuel to make it back to the mainland. Not on the rough sea. Possibly not on any sea.

He had no choice, then. They had to keep going, and find a place to hide—soon. Or Viktor could catch up to them on the open water. Then all Bosch would need to do was fight them off their precarious perch on the Jet Ski. Their exhaustion and the weight of their body armor would do the rest.

There was little other option. Of the many islands stretching out toward the open sea, the only one that offered any place to hide was Dorsi. Kirk cringed at the idea of leading Viktor to the ancient fortress, especially since he knew Bosch had been seeking the scepter of Charlemagne. Even if, by some chance, Thad hadn't left the scepter on the island, Viktor could easily uncover enough clues in the old castle to ultimately lead him to the Lydian heir and the scepter.

But Dorsi was nearly unapproachable. The only decent spot to anchor was the hidden inlet, and that was tricky enough to find. He and Thad had even had difficulty finding it the first time, and that was with a map to guide them. It wasn't something anyone was likely to stumble upon, certainly not in the thrashing seas they slogged through.

If he could shake Viktor just long enough to make a break for the inlet, he might be able to escape without detection. And in that respect, Dorsi was a perfect choice. A strand of keys lay just off the east side, in close enough proximity that, if he weaved among them quickly enough, he might leave Viktor in the shadow of an island while he and Stasi slipped away to safety.

He gunned the Jet Ski through the mounting waves. It was a long shot, but it was all he had.

\* \* \*

Stasi pinched her eyes shut and gripped the handlebars with all her strength. Though the waters of the Mediterranean were temperate in June, the rain that fell from the sky was much cooler, and the force of the wind around them chilled her. Already, uncontrollable shivers trembled through her, and it was all she could do to keep her teeth from chattering.

Surely Kirk knew what he was doing. She'd wanted so badly to hide at Channel Island, not because she thought it would be a safe choice, but simply because she was so exhausted. They had to rest soon.

A violent shiver chased up her spine, jarring her lungs, sending her into a sputtering fit of coughing. Between the waves and the drenching rain, her face had been assaulted by a near-constant onslaught of water. She'd breathed in far too much liquid, and it filled her stomach and her lungs.

Her lungs.

She'd always had to be careful to keep her lungs clear. They'd always been her weak point—prone to pneumonia and congestion. The constant deluge of water could prove to be more deadly than the enemy who pursued them.

At the thought of Viktor, Stasi blinked her eyes open and peered past Kirk's solid arms to the craft that hounded them. Viktor's fierce face cackled with malice, as though he knew that, one way or another, she and Kirk were done for.

Pressing her face into Kirk's arm, Stasi found she could breathe more easily in the shadow of his shoulder. Sucking in a few steady breaths, she tried to think. Kirk and his men had risked so much so that she could sign the covenant. All their efforts would come to nothing if she didn't make it back to Sardis alive. They'd come so far and sacrificed so much.

Coughing out more seawater, Stasi struggled to catch her breath, to urge Kirk on. They couldn't give up. Not yet.

She prayed that God would keep them safe. That somehow—in spite of the bleak situation, God would rescue them from Viktor, and from all those who opposed the crown.

But how?

Peering out past Kirk's arm, she saw the last islets of the Sardis keys flash past. There was nothing left but the Island of Dorsi and the open sea. Kirk pointed the Jet Ski toward the Dorsi inlet and gunned it to top speed.

What was he thinking? If they led Viktor to Dorsi, Thad's hideout would be exposed. They couldn't afford to give away where he'd been hiding! If their enemies knew Thad was still alive, they wouldn't stop until they tracked him down. Worse yet, if Thad had left the scepter hidden on the island, Viktor might find it!

Kirk slipped in through the rocks that rimmed the island, narrowly avoiding their jutting forms as their craft careened toward the hidden opening that led to the secret inlet. She pulled her knees tight to the Jet Ski, barely missing scraping against the jagged reef. The heaving waves tossed them forward like a toy boat, and moments later beached them high on the sand.

Kirk peeled himself off the craft and lifted her off after him.

She tried to thank him, to say anything, but her teeth chattered with such uncontrollable force no words came out. Stumbling after him up the beach, she found she was too weak to protest when he hoisted her into his arms and carried her up the familiar path that led to the queen's tower.

Once inside the small covered room, Stasi found she could catch her breath. Rain still drummed on the stone structure all around them, but in the ancient enclosed space, everything was dry. Water poured in rivulets from her clothes, pooling on the floor.

Kirk opened the stone compartment where many of Thad's things were hidden and pulled out a blanket, tucking it around her shoulders before pulling her into his embrace. "Are you going to make it?"

"Y-y-yes," she chattered, still shivering convulsively. "Do you think we'll be safe here?"

"I hope so." Kirk let go of her shoulders and crossed to the narrow arrowslit window that overlooked the inlet. His face blanched.

"Did he follow us?"

"He just beached his Jet Ski." Kirk crossed to Thad's small arsenal of supplies. "It won't take him long to find us. We've got to be ready."

# SIXTEEN

Stasi rummaged through the bin with shaking fingers. Thaddeus had left many items stowed away, but what use were a spyglass and a sleeping bag against the heartless enemy who was likely carrying more than one gun? Fighting back a cough, she noticed Kirk's lips were moving, and she slid close enough to hear his words.

"Dear God, protect us."

She found the superpowerful emergency parachute her brother had invented. Maybe they could climb to the top of the tower and parachute away? She tucked it under her arm and grabbed another item. Thad's crank flashlight. Right. Maybe she could shine it in her enemy's eyes and blind him?

A despairing sob escaped her lips.

"None of that." Kirk had some sort of sword in a scabbard. He grabbed her hand.

She glanced through the arched doorway and saw Viktor quickly climbing the winding stairs.

Kirk tugged her in the direction of the stairs leading to the battlement with its crenellated parapets. They reached the flat landing that towered at least twenty meters above the rest of the island. The rain continued to fall, pooling in slick puddles, sometimes several centimeters deep.

"Don't get too close to the wall," Kirk cautioned her. "Some of these old stones are loose."

Stasi nodded and prayed as she gulped a breath for courage.

Then Viktor burst onto the open tower, and Kirk stepped in front of her, brandishing the sword he held.

Viktor drew his gun.

With a flick of his wrist, Kirk knocked the weapon from Viktor's hand, and the shot went wild. The gun flew free of the turret, rattling down the stone wall.

Stasi never heard it hit the bottom.

Leaping sideways past Kirk, Viktor lunged at her, and Stasi clutched the items she'd carried and ducked out of the way just as Viktor swung his leg in a wide kick.

Stasi threw the flashlight at the man's head, momentarily stunning him, and sending a trickle of blood streaming down his cheek with the rain.

Kirk leaped onto Viktor's back, tearing him away, but even as he pulled the man backward, Viktor kicked out again, this time catching her with his boot under her jaw.

Stars exploded behind her vision as Stasi's head snapped back. She tried to shake off the blow, to counter in some way, but it was all she could do to get her eyes open in time to see another boot flying toward her face.

Then there was nothing but pain, and the stone floor beneath her.

Stasi blinked past the agony and forced her eyes to open. What had happened? She heard Kirk's voice, but the sound seemed to have come from somewhere far away, beyond the turret.

She strained to see through the falling rain. Viktor stood by the far parapet, leering.

"Tell me where the scepter is!" Viktor shouted. "I know

he took it! You've got three more seconds before I pry your fingers from the wall and you fall to your death. And who will save your princess then?"

With a jolt of clarifying anger, Stasi realized that the loose stones of the crenel had fallen away, and Kirk apparently clung to the remaining ledge, with Viktor plying him for information, determined to kill him.

Stasi had no doubt that, even if Kirk told the man everything, Viktor would kill him. He'd kill them both, or kill Kirk and turn her over to her enemies.

"No!" Stasi shouted. She raised herself up to a sitting position and blinked back the stars that followed. Her shout had caught the attention of Viktor, and his hand still hovered in the air.

"I thought I'd killed you already." Viktor took a menacing step in Stasi's direction.

Through pain-filled vision, Stasi spotted her brother's emergency parachute, which had fallen next to her in her skirmish. She grabbed it up and was about to throw it at the man when she spotted the release button.

With little time to think beyond the possibility of the open parachute catching Kirk, or possibly giving him some means to climb back up onto the battlement, she aimed the pack at Bosch and squeezed the button with her thumb.

The force of the ejecting parachute threw her back against the parapet behind her, and more stars erupted from her vision. She wavered, half expecting Viktor to hit her again at any moment. Instead, she heard the distant rattle of something falling down the steep sides of the tower.

"Kirk!" She scrambled across the wet stones on her hands and knees. Had he fallen? Her heart tore at the thought of losing him, and she realized she'd never gotten the chance to tell him that she loved him.

She reached the edge of the tower. What remained of

the crumbled section of parapet was less than a meter high. Clasping the side of the thick wall, she pulled herself up onto her knees, and saw fingers holding tight on the other side.

"Kirk!"

"Help me up," he panted, and pain labored across his features.

The nylon ropes of the ejected parachute dangled just past him. Stasi wrapped the pack tightly around a solid crenel and pulled the rope into a tight knot. "Can you grab the rope?"

Kirk got hold of it with both hands and, with her straining from the top end, he inched his way over the edge.

"Careful of your ribs," she reminded him as he winced in pain.

Kirk rolled onto his side as he crawled over what was left of the stone wall.

"Are you all right?" Stasi gathered his face into her hands. The rain had mostly died down, and far to the west the sinking sun broke through the clouds, sending golden rays of light streaming down.

"Better," he panted. "Better now."

"I'm so glad." She bent her face to his and planted a tentative kiss on his lips. When she began to pull away, he rose up slightly after her.

She kissed him again. "I never got to tell you. I love you."

The smile fled from his eyes, replaced by a wary look.

His response stabbed at her. Did he not feel the same way? The previous kiss they'd shared seemed to indicate so, but his grim expression told her otherwise.

He eased himself to a sitting position. "I should retrieve the body before it gets dark."

"Body?"

"Viktor's. There's no way he could have survived that fall, even if the impact from the chute didn't get him. Judging from what it did to the fountain statue years ago, I'd say he was likely dead before he ever hit the ground."

"I killed him?" Remorse stabbed through her. Granted, he was a horrible person who'd tried to kill them both. And there would have been awful repercussions if Viktor told anyone what he'd seen on Dorsi, or worse yet, found the scepter. But at the same time, the thought that she'd taken a human life cut at her heart.

"The chute killed him." Kirk gave her a solemn look. "You didn't do it on purpose. But still, I'm glad you did it. He made it clear it was us or him." He groaned as he got to his feet, steadying his ribs with one hand as he made his way to the steps.

Stasi followed him down the stairs to the queen's chamber. "How are we going to get back to Sardis? The Jet Ski won't have enough fuel to make it back."

"This." Kirk pulled an object from Thad's storage bin, and held it up for her to see. A long piece of plastic tubing dangled from something that looked like a cross between an air pump and an enormous perfume atomizer.

"Another of Thad's inventions?" Stasi looked the bulbous thing over, wondering how it was going to transport them across fifty kilometers of open sea.

"It's a siphon. We can move the gas from the other craft all into our tank. It may not get us all the way to Sardis, but it will get us most of the way. We'll take an oar and row into port if we have to."

By the time Kirk got the gas siphoned, the sun was setting and the cloudy sky was dark.

"Let's not worry about fetching the body right now." Stasi shivered against the relentless cold. Kirk had bundled her in a blanket, but she'd been shivering for too long to stop now.

His gentle hand cupped her cheek. "You're right. I need to get you to town."

With that, they climbed on the Jet Ski and headed off into the sunset.

Stasi pinched her eyes shut and let Kirk steer. She felt so exhausted, and her constant shivering convinced her she likely had caught a fever. They slipped past several islands before Kirk began to wave and shout.

"What is it?" Stasi looked ahead to see a boat approaching them, with smiling faces eagerly waving back.

"Linus and Jason," Kirk explained. "Looking for us."

They motored alongside the larger boat and clambered in, attaching the Jet Ski so they could tow it back to port behind them. Stasi was glad to be off the tiny craft and onto something steadier. The men brought her more blankets and hot chocolate, which she sipped while she slumped against Kirk on a bench seat.

"Viktor Bosch's body is on the island of Dorsi," Kirk explained to the men.

"How did he die?" Linus asked.

Jason chided his friend. "Don't you know? No one visits the island of Dorsi and returns alive."

"That's right." Kirk gave them both a stern look of affirmation. "We'll have to go back out later and recover his body."

"We can take care of that. You need your rest," Jason told him.

"Who's going to be the head of the royal guard with Bosch out of the picture?" Linus asked.

"Jason is eligible for the job. And he's the highest-ranking officer who has demonstrated allegiance to the crown." Kirk nudged Stasi gently. "Would you like to appoint him?"

Stasi looked up through bleary eyes at the men who'd done so much to protect her. "Gladly. And Linus can have Jason's vacated position."

The man gave a shout, and Stasi startled. "Is it a promotion? It was intended to be."

"A promotion and a raise." Linus laughed happily. "Thank you, Your Highness."

As they neared the city, the men radioed ahead, and Galen met them at the marina. Stasi felt too weak to stand, and couldn't stop shivering.

"Her fever's getting bad," Kirk murmured to the others. "Let's take her straight to the hospital."

Stasi didn't argue with them. She didn't have the strength, but let Kirk carry her to a car and then into the hospital in Sardis.

The ringing phone woke her. She was somewhere warm and comfortable. Stasi looked around, recognized her surroundings as a hospital room, found the phone next to her bed and answered it.

"Juliet?"

"Uh." Stasi's sleepy mind churned into gear. "Yes." And what was Thad's code name again? "Is this Regis?"

"It is. I had to call and tell you how proud I am of what you did yesterday."

Stasi tried to think of what, out of all the things she'd done the day before, he might be proud of. Killed a man? Nearly gave away his hiding place?

"You kept our family's stake in the throne."

Oh, yes, that. Maybe she had done something to be proud of after all. She found her voice. "Thank you. And I'm proud of you, too."

"For what?" Thad sounded sincerely surprised. "Running away?"

"For refusing to be a part of something unethical."

"I kick myself sometimes. I should have stayed to protect you."

"You made the right choice. And you didn't leave me alone. You left your friend—what's his code name?"

"Romeo."

Stasi squeezed her eyes shut tight. Yes. She should have guessed it.

"You don't mind that I gave the two of you coordinating names, do you?"

"He minds."

Thad laughed. "That's half the fun of it. He always denied how he felt for you, but it was always there, just the same. I knew I could trust you to him."

Stasi's heart squeezed.

"Is everything all right?" Thad asked.

"I don't know if he feels what you think he feels."

Thad laughed again. "Give him some time. I'll be watching the papers for an announcement."

Before Stasi could object and say there would never be an announcement, Thad continued.

"I should go. Give my love to the family."

Stasi fumbled through a goodbye and hung up the phone, staring at it a long minute before deciding to get on with her day. She spotted a familiar bag on the chair across the room and found it contained her travel things that Theresa always kept packed for her. The small en suite bathroom had a shower, and Stasi quickly freshened up before dressing.

When she came back into her room, she startled at the sight of Kirk sitting in the lone chair.

"Have you been here long?"

"Just arrived. Thought I'd wait."

Stasi froze midway across the room, unsure whether to throw herself into his arms or casually take her place perched on the bed opposite him.

He must have sensed her uncertainty, because he stood and took a step closer to her. "Are you all right?"

"I'm feeling better. How did everything turn out? Did the body get retrieved?"

"Yes."

"He was dead?"

"Quite dead." Kirk took another step closer. "It was for the best. Viktor shot your father yesterday."

"What? When?"

"It happened at the Hall of Justice just as we were leaving."

"Is he okay?"

"He's here at the hospital. He came through surgery just fine, but he's still in a coma. They say that's the best thing for him, so his body can focus on repairing itself."

"Oh, Kirk." Stasi closed the last space between them and found herself in the comfort of his arms. "My poor father. I know he made some wrong choices, but I believe he was trying to make up for them."

"That's the way I understand it. If he hadn't taken that bullet, you may never have gotten out of the Hall of Justice alive."

Stasi rested her cheek on Kirk's chest, holding him tight as she absorbed the sacrifice her father had made to protect her. "Now what's going to happen to the monarchy?"

"You and your sister signed the covenant. So did David Bardici."

"But I thought he was implicated in the conspiracy with the insurgents?"

"Until we have direct evidence to charge him, he remains eligible to be a part of the ruling council. But the good news is, since both you and your sister signed the agreement, you have majority representation. You accomplished what needed to happen. Perhaps Alexander will find his way back, and then he can sign the covenant, as well. In the meantime, your family can move back into the palace."

"Are you and your parents moving back to the cottage?"

"Actually—" his expression sobered "—I've been trying to convince them to move back to Georgia with me."

Stasi pulled away and looked him in the face, surprised. "You're moving to America? For how long?"

"It would be a permanent move."

She felt as though all the breath had been stolen from her weakened lungs. "Why? Is it because of the upheaval in Lydia?"

"No. In fact, if I'm needed here, I could stay until your family reclaims the throne. But then I need to get away."

"I don't understand."

"Your Highness." Kirk reverted to using her formal title, and took a step back from her. "I need to distance myself from you. My interactions with you were inappropriate. You're a princess. I'm nothing—"

"You aren't *nothing*," Stasi cut him off. "You saved my life. I owe you everything. Lydia owes you—"

"It doesn't matter. I need to go." He took a step toward the door.

With a little leap, Stasi cleared the space between them, got her arms around his shoulders and kissed him.

For a half second he froze, as though he wanted to resist, but then he gave in to her kiss, wrapping his arms around her and lifting her up, returning her kisses with increasing affection.

Then he pulled away like a drowning man gasping for breath. "*This* is why I must leave."

"I love you," Stasi whispered.

"I shouldn't." He shook his head sorrowfully and ran his fingers through her hair. "I shouldn't love you."

"But you do?"

"More and more every day. I love you, Stasi. I've got to go, for your sake and mine."

As Kirk spoke, Queen Elaine stepped through the open door and cleared her throat.

Kirk dropped his arms and stepped away from Stasi.

"Oh, Mother!" Stasi took a second to regain her composure, then recalled the items still tucked into her travel bag. "The crown jewels." She scooped them up and presented them to her mother. "They're rightfully yours."

"I sent them to you. They're yours now."

Before Stasi could object, the queen turned to Kirk. "As a token of our family's thanks for all you've done for Stasi, I present you with this." She held out a ring, its large central diamond surrounded by teardrop amethysts, so that it looked like a flower in bloom. "The ring of the crown jewels. Although it should stay with the rest of the set." She gave them both a meaningful look.

Kirk's eyes widened.

Queen Elaine cleared her throat. "Thaddeus always said you were the only man he'd ever trust with his sister. The king and I agree." Then she leaned closer to Kirk and whispered, "The ring is just the right size for Stasi's left ring finger."

Kirk shook his head. "I don't deserve—"

"Hush." Elaine pressed the ring into his hand. "I'll have none of that. You are a noble man. Your character defines who you are, not some title. You saved my daughter's life. All of Lydia owes you."

Looking back and forth between the queen and Stasi, Kirk looked as though he fought an inner battle. As a smile spread across his face, Stasi couldn't help smiling back.

Dropping to one knee, Kirk looked up at Stasi with as much fear in his eyes as she'd seen there at any time on their adventures of the last week. "Anastasia?"

"Yes?"

"Will you marry me?"

"Yes!"

He slid the ring onto her finger and she took his hand, pulling him back up to standing and into her arms. Then he kissed her until she forgot the troubles of the last week and the long journey ahead of them, and thought only of her joy at their future together.

\* \* \* \* \*

# ACKNOWLEDGMENTS

Thank you to my loving and supportive family, who insist they love frozen pizza, freeing me from cooking so I can write. I love you all!

Thanks also to my awesome friends whose insights contributed to the factual accuracy of this book. Special thanks to Lonny Douthit, my cousin who flies helicopters, who patiently tried to explain them to me. Any errors are mine, not his! And thanks to all the friends who chimed in on my efforts to name the crown prince—because of you, he is not Xerxes or Phineas or Arthur. Blessings. And let me not forget all those friends who supplied terms and words when my brain ran dry. Because of you, the-woman-behind-the-ticket-counter-who-sells-tickets-at-the-airport shall henceforth be known as a ticketing agent. Ah. So much better.

And special thanks to my editor extraordinaire, Emily Rodmell, for her insight, expertise, and patience with my frantic Friday-afternoon email barrages. Enjoy your weekend in peace—you've earned it!

Dear Reader,

On July 17, 1918, the royal family of Russia was murdered by forces of the Bolshevik secret police. Their fourth and youngest daughter, Anastasia, was rumored to have survived the attacks, and myths about her continued existence persisted in various forms until the positive identification of the remains of the last of the family members in 2007.

Hers was a tragic story. The tales of her possible survival captured the imagination of generations of people who wished the story could have had a happy ending. We cannot go back in time and change the way things were, but in writing this book, her family was often on my mind. In order to escape, Anastasia would have needed help from faithful friends.

Ultimately, that is what this book is about: the power of friendship and forgiveness. I hope you've enjoyed the story of Anastasia and her family. Please look for the forthcoming books in the Reclaiming the Crown series, which pick up the story with Stasi's older brothers, Alexander and Thaddeus.

God's blessings on your journey,
*Rachelle McCalla*

# Questions for Discussion

1. Kirk has a reputation for being the most hated man in Lydia. As the story goes on, we learn the truth about the events that led to him being labeled this way. Have you ever assumed someone was guilty, only to later learn they were more honorable than you thought? What does this teach you about your ability to judge guilt and innocence?

2. When the motorcade is ambushed and Stasi believes her parents have been killed, she regrets not having hugged them goodbye. Have you ever lost a loved one suddenly? Do you treat your loved ones differently knowing they could be taken from you unexpectedly at any time?

3. Kirk is attacked and beaten, but refuses to tell his torturers anything about where Stasi has gone. Consider these words from 1 Peter 2:19–24. Does Kirk's experience give you any insights into Christ's suffering on your behalf?

For it is commendable if a man bears up under the pain of unjust suffering because he is conscious of God. If you suffer for doing good and you endure it, this is commendable before God. To this you were called, because Christ suffered for you, leaving you an example, that you should follow in his steps. When they hurled their insults at him, he did not retaliate; when he suffered, he made no threats. Instead, he entrusted himself to him who judges justly. He himself bore our sins in his body on the tree, so that we might die to sins and live for righteousness; by his wounds you have been healed.

4. Stasi feels awkward binding up Kirk's injuries because doing so requires her to get close to him. But in spite of her discomfort getting close to a man she feels attracted to, she does her best to secure the bindings to prevent further injury. Do you think her behavior is appropriate under the circumstances? How do her feelings complicate the issue?

5. Kirk is used to being strong and doing what needs to be done. Because of his injuries, he has to let Stasi sail his boat. Likewise, though Stasi has thus far been protected by Kirk, in sailing his boat, she must go beyond her comfort zone. Who do you most identify with in this scene? Do you need to allow others to help you more? Or do you need to step up and help?

6. Though Stasi hasn't spoken to Kirk in six years, he and his family risk their lives to help her. Have you ever received help you felt you didn't deserve? Do you find it easier to be the person who gives help, or the person who receives help? How can you respond to the generosity of others with grace?

7. Growing up, Kirk's parents told him repeatedly that Stasi was out of his league. How did their words influence his relationship with Stasi? How did their influence change over the course of time? Do you feel their words were helpful or hurtful? Why?

8. When they reach Georgia, Stasi longs to belong there and live a simpler life. Do you have roots in more than one place? How can you honor both? Do you feel Stasi's choices respect her heritage as both a country girl from Georgia and a princess?

9. Both Kirk and Stasi try to leave the other behind for their own safety. What does this tell you about the depth of their affection for one another? Have you ever had to distance yourself from someone you loved? How did things turn out for you?

10. Stasi's grandmother says, "There's nothing more important than our faith. If we keep tight hold of that, no enemy can touch us. Not really." What do you think she means by this statement? Do you agree with her words? How does her perspective give you courage when facing trials of your own?

11. King Philip made choices that contributed to the insurgent uprising, but in the end, he took a bullet for Stasi in an effort to make things right again. How do you feel about his character? Have you ever made a mistake and wished there was a way to make up for it? Did his sacrifice change anything?

12. Inside the locket, Stasi finds an inscription of Matthew 16:19: "I will give you the keys of the kingdom of heaven; whatever you bind on earth will be bound in heaven, and whatever you loose on earth will be loosed in heaven." Why do you feel this verse was chosen for the inside of the locket? How does its use here match its use in the Bible? How is it different?

13. In order to prevail against their enemies, Kirk and Stasi had to make many decisions about who they could trust, often with little time to deliberate the pros and cons. What basis did they use for making these judgments? How do you make split-second decisions about trusting others?

14. Even though Prince Thaddeus is not able to be with his family, he contributes to their protection through Kirk and through his inventions, which help Stasi and Kirk overcome their attackers and reach the safety of the mainland. How do you support and protect your family when you can't be with them?

15. Stasi and Kirk both had feelings for each other from a young age, even though they refused to act on those feelings until they were much older. How do you feel about their choices? Are they better or worse off for staying apart so long? Does their story give you any insights into your relationships or those of your loved ones? If so, what?

# INSPIRATIONAL

Wholesome romances that touch the heart and soul.

celebrating
15
YEARS

## COMING NEXT MONTH
### AVAILABLE MARCH 13, 2012

**EYE OF THE STORM**
Hannah Alexander

**THE DETECTIVE'S SECRET DAUGHTER**
*Fitzgerald Bay*
Rachelle McCalla

**BROKEN TRUST**
Sharon Dunn

**SHADES OF TRUTH**
*Undercover Cops*
Sandra Orchard

# REQUEST YOUR FREE BOOKS!

## 2 FREE RIVETING INSPIRATIONAL NOVELS
## PLUS 2 FREE MYSTERY GIFTS

*Love Inspired.*
# SUSPENSE

*Victoria Evans has come back to Fitzgerald Bay
after ten years, and she's got a secret that will affect
one of the Fitzgerald brothers greatly.
Read on for a sneak preview of
THE DETECTIVE'S SECRET DAUGHTER
by Rachelle McCalla, the next exciting book in the
FITZGERALD BAY series.*

A police cruiser tore up Main Street in Fitzgerald Bay, lights flashing.

Victoria Evans glanced back over her shoulder from the doorway of the Hennessy Law office. Who was in trouble now? She half expected the patrol car to stop in front of the police station, but it skidded to a halt on the other side of the street, and a uniformed officer leaped out, running toward the Sugar Plum Inn and Café.

"My shop!" Victoria turned to face Cooper Hennessy, handing off the frosted cookies she'd walked up the street to deliver. "Paige is in there."

Immediately afraid for her nine-year-old daughter's safety, Victoria leaped from the stoop and sprinted down the street, reaching her front door just as the police officer, who'd darted around the side of the building, circled back to the front.

Victoria reached for the door handle the same instant he did. Gloved fingers brushed her hands. She looked up past the broad shoulders to close-cropped brown hair. The handsome face turned toward her with eyes as blue as the Massachusetts sky. She knew those eyes too well.

"You can't go in there," the officer warned.

Her heart plummeted to her stomach. "But my daughter—"

"She's okay. She called 9-1-1. I don't want you contaminating the crime scene." He turned away and rushed inside.

Tumultuous emotions broke like waves inside her heart. She'd already had a crime scene at the Sugar Plum Inn and Café a few weeks before—an ugly break-in that had caused expensive damages.

What now? Was Paige really okay? Victoria had no family left besides Paige. She had to force herself to follow the officer's instructions not to go inside.

It didn't help who the officer was.

Owen Fitzgerald.

Of all the officers on the Fitzgerald Bay Police Department, why did Owen have to come? She couldn't have him finding out that he had a daughter this way.

*Can Victoria and Owen move beyond the past to build a future, or will she become the next target of the killer that is stalking Fitzgerald Bay?*

*Read THE DETECTIVE'S SECRET DAUGHTER by Rachelle McCalla to find out.*